BILLY O'CA

Billy O'Callaghan is the author of the critically acclaimed novel *My Coney Island Baby*, which has been translated into nine languages and was shortlisted for the Encore Award 2020. Stories in his short-story collection *The Boatman and Other Stories* were shortlisted for the Costa Short Story Award and for Writie.ie Short Story of the Year in the An Post Irish Book Awards. He lives in Douglas, a village on the edge of Cork City.

ALSO BY BILLY O'CALLAGHAN

(stories)
In Exile
In Too Deep
The Things We Lose, The Things We Leave Behind
The Boatman and Other Stories

(novels)
The Dead House
My Coney Island Baby

BILLY O'CALLAGHAN

Life Sentences

VINTAGE

1 3 5 7 9 10 8 6 4 2

Vintage is part of the Penguin Random House group of companies
whose addresses can be found at global.penguinrandomhouse.com

Penguin
Random House
UK

Copyright © Billy O'Callaghan 2021

Billy O'Callaghan has asserted his right to be identified
as the author of this Work in accordance with the
Copyright, Designs and Patents Act 1988

First published in Vintage in 2022
First published in hardback by Jonathan Cape in 2021

penguin.co.uk/vintage

A CIP catalogue record for this book is available from the British Library

ISBN 9781529112962 (B format)

Printed and bound in Great Britain by Clays Ltd, Elcograf S.p.A.

The authorised representative in the EEA is Penguin Random House
Ireland, Morrison Chambers, 32 Nassau Street, Dublin D02 YH68

Penguin Random House is committed to a sustainable future
for our business, our readers and our planet. This book is
made from Forest Stewardship Council® certified paper.

MIX
Paper from
responsible sources
FSC® C018179

LIFE SENTENCES

Family Tree

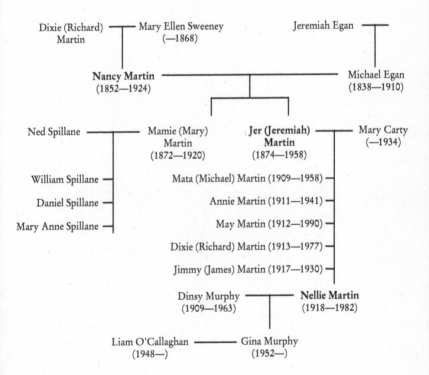

for Nan
with the greatest admiration

I

Jer

(1920)

I'd been in Barrett's pub since six, drinking fast and heavy. The few other men at the bar saw enough to keep to themselves, and though I had come straight from the fields, having spent the day since first light cutting grass for silage, and after the second pint had no more money in my pocket, the drink kept coming at me and I kept putting it away. A couple of hours in, I'd yet to feel the effect, and it was because of weariness finally, and maybe also because of a need to be alone, that I gave up my place at the counter and moved instead to the bench seat in shadow at the end of the lounge, with a table for my glass and the wall to support my back.

Around nine, the guards had entered. Looking for me.

I tried to tell them that whatever I'd said earlier at the bar meant nothing, that it was just the porter talking, but Tom Canniffe had been in the Munster Fusiliers with me, and the other two were old RGA men, gunners, and they knew. They knew me, but they also knew themselves, what they were capable of and what they'd have done had they been in my position, and it was Tom, the best of them and the least imposing, though only by degrees, who sat down opposite me and who put the cuffs on the table and asked, in a low voice, whether there was need for such things or if I was going to behave myself and come along quietly. Speaking in that murmur, as if from somewhere far away, looking at me but not meeting my stare, focusing instead on a point near my heart, while the other two, Larry Regan and Pat Hegarty, remained a couple of paces back on either side of him, relaxed but ready. Big men both, my size or near as be damned, Regan like a bull across the shoulders, Hegarty not so broadly set but with the look of iron about his bones; they had always been good company to sup a pint with or to play a game of cards or billiards in the Hall. But Tom and I had shared the trenches, and had shaken and bled alongside one another in Flanders and at Loos, and because they each had their own such bond with other men, they understood that it was necessarily different between the two of us.

'It's just the drink, I'm telling you, lads. There's no need for all this.'

'Sure, what else would you say?' Tom sighed, shaking his head. 'Porter talk is usually just different shades of shite. But every now and then it tells us something worth heeding. The problem for us is knowing which is which.'

'You can't keep me from my own sister's funeral, Tom,' I said. 'That's not right. In nobody's book is that right.'

4

'Sergeant.'

'What?'

'It's Sergeant now. You can't be calling me Tom. Not while I'm on duty. The uniform. You know how it has to be.'

I considered him, and the others. Five years earlier, as big and friendly as these three were, I'd have tried to kick my way out of the room, and they'd have had to beat me into splinters to stop me. But in the time since the war I'd thickened and turned slow, and sitting there at the back table of Barrett's lounge, this night of all nights, I felt as if I'd been knocked stupid by a shell. I suppose there are just times when the fight goes out of a man.

'It's for your own good,' he went on, still not meeting my eye, still not raising his voice above a rustling. 'It's not that we want this. Don't think that of us, Jer. Christ almighty, man. I'd be the same in your boots. But we cut you loose and, what? You go home and get a knife or a hatchet.'

I almost smiled, though happiness was a long way from my mouth.

'I'd have no need of a blade,' I said. My hands, flat before me on the table either side of my near-empty glass, pulled up into fists. 'Not for a fella like Ned Spillane. Put the pair of us on a quiet road and I'd beat him into the ground. I'd butter the stones with him.'

'Yeah,' said Tom. 'That's what I mean. That's what I'm talking about.'

All at once the air came out of me, and I felt my shoulders drop. 'Except I wouldn't,' I told them. 'He deserves every word of it and a time will likely come when he'll get it yet. From someone else if not from me. But tomorrow is for other things. The day's not about him. Mamie has to be buried right.'

'Don't make this worse than it needs to be,' one of the men behind Tom said. I lifted my stare from one to the other but for some reason couldn't decide which of them had spoken until Regan cleared his throat and added, in a different timbre: 'The Sergeant's right, Jer. Your word is solid with us. You know that. And we all accept that you mean what you say. But your man only has to come out with the wrong thing, or you'll see him sobbing at the graveside or collecting sympathies, and you'll snap. Not one of us here would blame you if you did, but if you go at him you'll be banged away, and that's just the fact of it. Maybe five years, maybe more, depending on how far you take it or if there's any stopping yourself once you've started. And no one wants that; not us, not you, and certainly not your wife and kids. The cell is all right for a night, and sure we'll sit up and chat with you if that's what you want, and we'll fill you with tea till you're sick of the stuff. This is the best way.'

'And if I refuse?'

Tom leaned in, and now his eyes did meet mine. For an instant we were lost again in the war, the two of us cowering down in the rubble of a destroyed cattle shed,

6

with everything tasting and smelling of France. Beneath the crack of remembered gunfire, we glimpsed once more the truth of one another, and we clung to that from either end as a kind of lifeline.

'Show a bit of sense, Jer,' he said. 'You were never the kind of man to start trouble when it could be avoided. And you were never stupid.'

'You don't know what you're doing to me, Tom. What you're taking. For a long time, there was only Mamie and me. I can't begin to describe the times we went through. And when they bury her tomorrow they'll be putting part of me into the ground, too. The best part. Christ, the wars I fought should have been for her. I should have gutted Spillane like a trout the very first time he glanced in her direction. Instead, I let it come to this.'

'Take it easy, Jer. He didn't kill her. Pleurisy, they're saying. There's plenty have died of that.'

'He killed her. He might not have kicked the chair away but with his drinking he put the rope around her neck. He's been killing her for years. And now she's gone.'

Across the table, Tom was still studying me. Then, all at once, he seemed to slacken. He reached out for the handcuffs, and passed them to Regan. 'It's early enough yet,' he said, without turning his head. 'There's time for a pint, I'd say, before we start heading back. Get them in, will you, Larry?'

*

Sometimes, when I'm alone and have a little time to ponder, I get to thinking about who I am. Not who I'm supposed to be, or trying or pretending to be, but my true self. Most of the time I keep that stuff blocked out, or buried way down, because it's not an especially healthy train of thought, but occasionally, when my mood turns reflective, I open my mind to it.

I'll be out walking in the fields at the top of Hilltown, with one of those pale springtime mornings on the slow rise, listening to the wind in the ironwoods and watching Snowy, my terrier pup, charge headlong into the furze, taunted into snarling chase by the flash of a passing hare or rabbit, only to re-emerge minutes later, whimpering and reddened in a thousand small places by the bush's green talons. Or I'll be lying in bed, with my wife Mary locked in sleep beside me and the gentle sounds of the children stretched out on sacking on their part of the floor, and I'll feel the night as a coffin's lid pinned down across me from head to foot, and my breath comes as slow as I can make it and tastes always in my mouth and throat of dust, steel and burnt trees and, beneath that, rotten flesh, and, down at the very bottom, screams. It is 1920, and nearly four years since the Somme, but the flavours of that fighting haven't left me.

Days, full of labour as they tend to be, limit time for reflection, and it is only above in those high Hilltown fields, or lying awake beneath the whole emptiness of night, that my mind is given ground to run. It has to do with the sweeping undulations of the land, and the flow of the sky above it. And it has to do with the deep, pulling gape of the small-hours air. With no work to hand, and nobody waiting on words, a man's head gets full, and those things that can never be talked about are the things that swamp the brain to overflowing. Such as, who I am. Such as, where I properly belong.

The best water comes from a long way down, and is washed clean by the rocks below us; the deeper the source, the surer we can be of its purity. And in a similar way, we know people first by their name, by their kin. As people, we value pedigree. And if the name is just a name, as mine is, without foundation or depth, then we cannot properly identify them. Without knowing who and where he comes from, a man is a mystery to himself.

In the barracks' cell, somewhere among the small hours, I sit slumped over with my elbows on my knees and my fingers laced loosely together in a way that would be prayerful on another man. These are rooms built for stillness, and restriction, the bare brick walls close on every side, and the solitary window does nothing but tease with its revelation of a starless sky, the narrow meshed box of glass giving a suggestion of the confessional. But I sit facing away, keeping all of that resolutely behind me. The only light is that of a kerosene lantern spitting dull glow from the office at the far end of the hallway, and exhaustion finally suffocates me, causing my mind to sink slowly from the man I appear to be, down to the stranger lying half an inch beneath the surface of my skin.

*

9

When I was a boy, I liked listening for the wind. Time has elevated that to the very sound of my childhood. Because I couldn't quite define its shape, I put my own shape to it, made an identity of the wind that was like my own but older, and I tried in every way I could to make sense of what that meant, where it came from. I spun a revenant from the many anonymous threads of myself, in an effort, I suppose, to create some sense of story, some lineage. The voice that filled the wind for me was never strong, but it was in some way familiar, like all those old songs I'd listened to and sort of knew. And searching as I was, I let myself believe that it was somehow the missing part of me, the part I'd been other-wise denied.

Even now, I see myself in shards of glass and find more of a sense of identity there than I can in the shaving mirror. Standing in the cold of an early morning in our backyard, staring at my reflection, the face I see in the rust-freckled glass is a strange one: flesh leaden with middle age; eyes wide in awe at having to fit myself, whoever I might be, to the tired features; skin lined by years and hanging from the scaffold of bone. The problem is that, with little knowledge of my family's line, I am largely foreign to myself.

There is a name in my head that has gone unspoken for so long. Michael Egan. I have a face in mind, too, thin and haggard, old-eyed, jaw like the corners of a headstone, that I've carried forward with me from my childhood, one that I'd seen on maybe half a dozen occasions over as many years and always somehow at a mile's remove, even when he and I found ourselves in the same room barely an arm's reach apart. A face I wanted to be able to love, and to have in my life and know, without fear. Eyes the waxy wood-grey colour of cloud ahead of heavy rain, watching me almost by accident; and a voice, when it came, all air, as vague as something poorly remembered or that old sighing of the wind, saying, *So you're Jer*, every time, every single time, as if confirmation were necessary, for both of us, in order to count as fact. *So you're Jer. Aren't you getting big. I hope you're being a good boy now for your mother.* And *Stand up straight, lad. The army won't have you if you're bent.* Other words too, and they're all inside me because I've saved them the way a starving bird will hoard scavenged crumbs, and when I can I take them out and repeat them, making the most of them, since they're what I have. I did this in the trenches too, and on the flat, grassy plains of Bloemfontein, our battalion marching with the last of our strength out of the burnt days and into some of the reddest sunsets any of us had ever seen. A few words, the same few, over and over, and features of a face that I've memorised so it's with me always. And that name. Michael Egan. Dead now, dead a long time, but one half of me then and still. I exist because of this man, but because of him I am also rootless. I made myself strong, in spite of him.

Life has given me what it's given to most people I've known: occasional spans of calm that serve only to connect and intensify the turmoil. The shades might differ, but that is all. I took my first breath in a work-house, the same as Mamie did. The Union, on the South Douglas Road, a place where everyone wept until tears stopped coming, and we were all prisoners of our circumstance until someone saw fit to turn us loose. Later on, we slept on straw, Mamie and I, huddled with our mother in corners of rat-infested tenement rooms, and ate whatever was going. There were plenty like us, we were not exceptional, and we did what it took to survive. Mamie was just two years older than me, but while we were very close as kids, you end up going where the road takes you. By the time I got out of the army – the first time, this was, back in '08, because I went in again when the Great War began – she was already married to Ned Spillane, with an infant in her arms and a second on the way. I'd known of them being together from the letters she sent, and also from the things that Mary wrote – Mary, who I was at that time courting and saving what few shillings I could put by in order to wed. The letters I received from both of them were crafted in a similar hand, slow and brittle, trying to fill me in on the happenings of the village, snippets of gossip that instead of making me feel I belonged somewhere, as was their intent, only underlined just how far away I was, in every respect, from those I loved. My poor mother would have written, too, every day if she could, had she ever learned how, but there were times when I gladly recognised her mark, a lopsided X scratched into the bottom of Mamie's

12

letters, in a way I chose always, though without logic or reason, to take as hopeful.

Ned Spillane was my own age, and for a few years of our childhood we'd lived within three doors of one another, along Bog View's lower terrace, on the edge of Douglas village. I remember his mother, Mrs Spillane, was a nice, harmless type of woman, who used to cut up the bread and butter, or jam if she had it, to share among whoever was playing rather than just singling out her own children. His family were the rooted ones, millworkers, the ones who properly belonged, while we were just the blow-ins, scraping together a pittance a week to take up some small amount of space in another family's home. I liked Spillane well enough then, in that way children tend to feel about other kids they grow up with, kicking a ball around a field or playing the games that boys play, fishing, climbing and fighting. Later on, once we'd reached our mid to late teens, we'd drink a few pints in each other's company over in Barrett's pub, and reminisce about the years we'd spent on Bog View, and the scutting we'd got up to, not just us but the whole gang of us, all the lads from our terrace. And once or twice, in Barrett's, I'd seen the ugly side of him in drink, spoiling for trouble and yet cute in his way, looking for it only with someone he might get the better of. But there were a few like that at sixteen, seventeen, and it never felt like something that could be held too hard against him. News of the marriage came as no shock to me, and because I'd been away such a long time, I remembered

13

Spillane as an all-right sort, maybe not one of those I was ever especially close to but decent enough. Reading his name in a letter, while sitting on my low bunk in the Aldershot barracks, brought old feelings out in me, my mind favouring the more gentle times, and though I'd likely have reacted differently had I been back in the village and at all aware of his appetite for drink, and how it caused him to behave, seeing such news put down on paper made it seem right somehow, a natural next step, and even stirred in me a kind of happiness.

But that was then. By the time I was stationed back in Cork, seconded to the Fermoy barracks for a few months before my discharge, the pair of them had already been to the altar and Mamie was again heavily pregnant. When I had a bit of leave, or a weekend pass after a three-night shift of sentry duty, I'd make the twenty-mile trip by train up into Cork city and then the tram the three miles more, out to Douglas. My main plan, I'll admit, was always to call on Mary and, if the weather was fine and she wasn't exhausted from her day's work at the woollen mill, to coax her into going for a walk, up past the Finger Post and along the Carrigaline Road where the alder and downy birch trees wrapped in above us like the ceiling of some old chapel, and it was secluded enough for her to dare take my hand, free from the embarrassment of being seen. But with time to pass until the mill's hooter sounded an end to Mary's working day, I'd stop at Spillane's house on Bog View to visit Mamie and my

14

mother, armed with some small gift of sugar or cake or a tin of golden syrup, and whatever shillings I had been able to put by for them. We'd sit for an hour or two then, drinking tea at the small table, the three of us chatting while Mamie's first little boy, William, was sleeping. I can see them that way still: Mamie smiling, or trying to smile, the strain of her pregnancy drawing the colour from her face; and our mother sitting close to me, neck sunk between her shoulders, clutching my hand and clinging tightly to the moments of our reunion, saying over and over whenever a pause opened up in our conversations, *my fine man, my fine big strong son.*

I was glad to be there, glad to be back, though I can't say that I much liked what I saw. Mamie looked tired, worn down in a way that could not be explained merely by her pregnant state, or by the infant in her care. Her eyes, always so bright and alive, had grown full of shadows. My mother caught me watching and answered me with a silent stare of her own, a warning look that I'd known on her forever, and when Mamie had risen to check on the baby, or to cut up the donkey's gudge that I'd sometimes bring from Thompson's bakery, she leaned in and put me in my place.

'They're fine as they are, Jer,' the scraping in the words giving her an intensity that I couldn't ignore. 'Don't interfere. Do you hear me, boy? Don't be coming between a husband and a wife. You've no business.'

She meant it, too, that being the way of things, a cruel unwritten law generally considered sacrosanct. And as time went on, as I finished up with soldiering and moved back to Douglas, married and started a family of my own, I did what I was told. I stayed back and watched as my mother's words turned all kinds of wrong and Mamie grew numb from life with a drunkard and the struggle to rear children on scraps that couldn't be spent on porter. And she began to drift from the world. If I happened across Spillane, I nodded hello in return to his salute, keeping the peace, but resisted any informality. And on those occasional afternoons when the weather brought work to an early finish and I wandered into Barrett's and found him the only customer at the bar, I'd refuse with a shake of my head his offer of a pint, even when it was clear enough that, due to a bit of luck with cards or a win on the dogs, he had the wherewithal and I had not. I was civil but largely silent, and tried to keep from listening or looking his way while he ran his mouth. If he was still sober he'd take the hint and quieten down, knowing better than to challenge me, and after that pint or the next one, some span of time long enough that he didn't feel he was losing face, he would push himself back from the counter and mumble a half-worded departure, and I'd nod and watch him leave for another watering hole, to empty out his pockets in one of the dockside pubs in Cork city.

Others knew the score between us, but nobody dared speak of it, realising I suppose that I was wound tight and that a wrong word would have set me off. And while they'd all have felt as I did in my situation, few enough of them would have sided with me had I gone at him in a way he deserved. Like I've said, that being the way of things.

Somewhere in the mix of that I became involved with Mary, one of the Cartys from along the Passage Road, half a mile or so from the Finger Post. The sister of one of our neighbours, and someone I'd known since I was a boy, she was multiples better than I could ever hope to be, and lifted me to a height whenever she uttered my name. We married in 1908 after three years of courting, and she moved in with my mother and me at Forge View, and in the years that followed reared a family that made me endlessly proud even when they weren't always good. Life had its struggles but we bore them in the way that our kind always do. I could say that I learned how in the trenches, but long before France or Africa I'd had my share of battles, so it'd be more correct to call it an instinct for survival.

War is something I know. Maybe the one thing I know well. In France they had us on the butcher's block from the start, yet Étreux, our piece of the Mons retreat, was just a warming-up for worse to come: at Givenchy, where we lost two hundred men in the first ten minutes; and again at Aubers Ridge, which made pieces of us, wiping out two-thirds of our number; and all of that ahead of the Somme. By then I'd already turned forty, and particularly through that autumn and the Loos winter of 1915, I was frozen with the cold. We all were. Rain fell like it had forgotten how to stop, and we marched to keep the madness at bay and because that was what we were ordered to do. Reasons as good as any, and a sight better than most. I often think about that time, of being back there, pressed against the face of a trench, up to my shins in grey water, with my eyes clenched shut, listening to the deep and oddly gentle rumblings of the gunners harassing the line with big shells not a hundred yards ahead of us, and having to kick the rats away throughout the night, some of them bigger than kittens rebounding against my legs in splashing flurries, their minds blind with confusion at how little distinguished those of us still living from the dead. And I remember their squeals, tiny insane battle howls, when I'd connect with a kick or step on one in the dark. During those days and nights in Loos, when the fighting was heavy, life as it should be simply ceased to exist, so that there was only this: a shelled town and shredded countryside, everything stinking of mortar and mustard gas, us on one side of the wreckage and the enemy splayed out along the other, none of us men any more, none of us human, no longer thinking of home and the faces of loved ones and happier days, but full instead of the things we'd seen and done and were doing still. We'd dug in, and amassed casualties faster than they could be buried, and on one of the mornings, when dawn arrived cold and the colour of cinders, the unit medic went to check on our wounded and discovered that rats had eaten away half the face of a soldier who'd taken shrapnel to the chest. We'd all heard the moans, but they'd by then become the sound of our nights, and when there was nothing that could be done, we learned to ignore them. I went with a few others to see for myself, knowing better but going anyway, because I'd heard about such things happening but never really believed them, never wanted to, and the soldier on his stretcher was still alive and according to the medic would likely survive, assuming he could make it to a hospital before infection set in. But the high dose of morphine had kept him stupid, dreaming awake, so that he was both there and a thousand miles removed, his mind back home in Limerick or Tipperary or wherever he'd come from, and with nobody available through the late hours to man the trench's infirmary corner, rats had massed on him and begun to feast. Fixating on the pliable, his lips and nostrils, cheeks and the easy parts of his ears, they'd caused quick ruin. Then they had chewed away his lids and gone for the pulpy treasure of his eyes. An hour on from dawn, in the clotted light, the effects of the narcotic began to ebb, and the soldier started to moan and then, within a minute, to roar, keening from the smashed chest, like something bestial caught in a snare. And I looked on, paled into silence, alongside the others who'd gone to see because, as bad as the sound was, what really did for us was the visual. Some men wept, the tears striping clean paths down their faces, though I didn't, because I'd by then learned that for a soldier it never helps. But just because I didn't cry didn't mean I didn't feel, and this was yet another of those sights which, once absorbed, can never be fully expelled. I've seen nuns mowed down by raking machine-gun fire, children set alight to burn away like candles, and looked into the eyes of men and boys as I fired on them from five feet away, and others, in Africa, as I sliced them open and trampled them during bayonet charges. I've seen war up close, felt the hot bloody mist of it on my face and hands, in my eyes and on my lips, and anyone who's been to battle knows that we all carry the consequences. We're none of us excused the marks of it.

The steely ringing of the nearby church bell rouses me from my reverie, slow chimes tolling the last of the day. The final note seems to linger, making the silence that follows less empty somehow. After listening hard for something more, I take off my boots and stretch out on the narrow bed, disturbed by the turn my thoughts have taken. A few hours of incarceration won't break me, but I wouldn't want to give it longer, locked away with nothing else to do but think. Darkness makes everything too clear, and remembering is just nourishment to pain. But if my mind is not in the past, it's raging with thoughts of Spillane, and the wretched life he gave Mamie. The loathing I have for my brother-in-law is in significant portion anger at myself, stoked by guilt for having behaved too well, for having listened to my mother and my wife, when told and pleaded with not to interfere. And while they had their own fears to balance, I should have been stronger. There'd have been consequences but nothing that I couldn't have faced, because my poor sister's was a life worth saving, and the least I should have done was try. Spillane was an animal in drink, but he wasn't all the way stupid, and he might have responded to a warning, a threat, something put in the right kind of menacing tone. One way or another, I should have acted. And now it is too late.

My wife Mary is devout, but this is a condition that's easier for women, I think, than for men. The women I've known tend to have stronger hearts, maybe because they are tuned to pain in ways that men can never be. Or maybe theirs is a different variety of pain. Women, in my experience, are more forgiving, and I think more hopeful, which only sets them up again and again for more of the same. Most of the men I've known are damaged things, and women have accepted that and found ways of handling our sharpest corners with care and caressing them to softness. The contradicting qualities of such a nature, the strength and the supplication, the ability to quietly conduct the ragged chorus of a family's day, are the very qualities that allow them to keep onto faith. And faith, in turn, steels them when hurt threatens to overwhelm.

My own contradictions twist me towards a different outlook. I do occasionally pray, if only for consolation, because as much as I might wish it otherwise, religion runs through me like the rings striping the innards of a tree. But lying here tonight I've learned that it is possible to pray – if that's what this is – and find some small comfort in the words, without having to believe. You get to that point, with doubt a kind of slowly creeping rot until a night comes when you are face down in a field or sitting, as now, in some jail cell, and you learn that the pleas dribbling imploringly from your mouth are flushed with wasted air, because whether God exists or not it's obvious that He can't hear, is helpless to intervene or simply doesn't care a damn for you. This isn't a lesson I could have been taught in words; it's a realisation I had to reach in my own time. But for me, it simplifies everything. The idea of an almighty, all-seeing God is too suggestive of grand plans and greater schemes, reasons that lie outside my comprehension; and thinking too much about that, why horrors happen and are allowed to happen, would, if I let it, turn me hateful until that becomes all I am. And I just feel that, if I am to go on, it is better to spare myself that burden.

I spoke about this once, briefly, with a priest, a man who'd been to some of the same places I've been to, and he confessed to me that he no longer believed either, at least not in any conventional way. Yet he remained a priest, letting ritual be his guide and finding comfort in that routine, and he could still bear the thought of God, and still retained it as something of worth because, as he saw it, it was about choosing what you needed to get by. I remember him saying that when the night turns still, what keeps us awake, what haunts us, are the things we've done more so than the things we've had done to us.

This was back in 1916, November coming into December, and I was on my way to Fishguard, having left Aldershot, and had boarded a train at Basingstoke. Trying to get home and, for some reason, nervous about it. The war was still without an end in sight, but after being wounded out from the Somme in mid-July my part was done. I'd already taken a hit prior to that, at Givenchy, the first week of '15, catching a fragment of shell across the outer side of my left thigh – just a quarter of an inch wide of costing me the leg, one medic said – which put me down for a few weeks' recuperation, before I rejoined the line ahead of Aubers Ridge. But this was the gas, an altogether different kind of damage, a flooding that burned me right through and had me nine days blind. In the field hospital and later on, once they got me back through the lines to Abbeville, I was only one of hundreds like me. Turned onto my side so that I wouldn't drown in my own juices, smothered out of all sound save for feeble gasps, I was certain I had fallen into hell. But all things pass, and once I could see again I knew I'd go on, though a part of me was not sure I should.

The priest had been on the train since London and was heading for Swansea, where he had a sister. It was early, a distance yet from daylight, and I'd been up most of the night, packing, preparing, talking myself into whatever life had next in store. The prospect of coming back

23

out into the world was daunting, the fear in its way as real as any felt when facing into battle. Your love for those people awaiting you, wife, mother, children, doesn't wane but you do wonder whether they'll have changed, or if you have, and you dread the possibility of finding yourselves strange and awkward with one another. I sat with the priest because I recognised the soldier in him. War hangs heavy on some men, and it has to do with the stillness they hold on to just as much as the wounds they are forced to carry. I was seated opposite him for a while before realising that he bore more obvious evidence of his conflict, and by then it was too late to change seats, even if I'd wanted to. His right arm was shrunken to a child's size – the limb shattered at the bone, he explained, three inches above the elbow by a German bullet. At Loos, in late September of the previous year, the 27th, eight thousand British dead in four hours and two and a half times that number over the three days of the offensive. I hadn't noticed the injury at first because of how he was leaning with that shoulder against the window and the way in which he had a newspaper unfurled across his lap. When his arm lifted into view I stared, unable to help myself, and he watched me with a calm that was too comfortable. The medics had wanted to amputate, he said, his voice almost lost against the thrum of our carriage on the old uneven track. Made blunt by the relentlessness of their work, they told him in French and uncertain English that the wound could never heal and would forever hurt. If he'd been less lucid they'd have just gone ahead and cut, without discussion, and he'd have woken up so much the better for that. But his stubbornness won out, and in the end they had actually smiled, to hear the foul-mouthed ease with which he argued his case, he sitting there in a filthy tent, his uniform sleeve cut away to the shoulder but his collar still in place at his throat and his rosary beads clenched in his good fist. The arm now was his penance, he said. A warning, too, against future stupidity, and vanity, and thinking that his contrary opinion mattered a damn in the face of expert assurances.

When we got to talking about faith, somewhere around Bristol, he said that he didn't put his own hurt down to God, at least not in the way I or anyone else might have assumed, because in his mind that was no longer what God was for. After wading through so much of France, he'd come to see the Almighty in a new light. He sighed, considered the ghost of his own reflection chalky in the train window's glass, and murmured that there were some who still continued to believe that God drags the sun up into the sky of a morning, and marks the sparrow's fall. But those were mostly the ones who hadn't had to suffer the Somme or Ypres or Gallipoli. For him, now, God or whatever you wanted to call It was a method of unburdening, a tool for convincing himself that he'd been forgiven those sins too terrible to speak of. Life, he said, speaking as much to his ghost in the glass as to me, was a daily attrition, for men, women and children just as much as for the birds in the trees and the rats in the ditches. The most anyone could ask for was survival, and whether those who succeeded in that counted as fortunate or accursed was a call each one of us had to make for ourselves.

I'd listened, thinking that there was some truth in his words, though for me it couldn't be that simple. My existence would find a new ease if I too could heap all of my sins onto God's strong back. But that's not who I am. I can't escape or deny the terrible things I know. The sights I've seen in war, and the way the workhouse dormitory from my earliest childhood – as much imagined as remembered and yet somehow no less real for that – sank into blackout after the lanterns had been blown, are ingrained in me. And I don't feel that such experiences should be forgotten. I wish they hadn't happened, but I am not seeking absolution for the things I've seen, done and suffered. The sleepless nights are occasional, and strangling as they can be, I see them as the price of a life's journey. Considered as a whole, from the day of my birth to this night in the barracks, the notion of God seems incidental to all I've known. Whether He exists or not is of no consequence, and changes nothing.

To keep from worrying too much about such things, I focus on the days. Waking to the thrill of a clean breath, and pushing the bad dreams back into the silence, overcoming all that has gone before. Getting up early to wash and shave in the backyard; savouring the ache in my arms and back on the slow walk home after the threshing or ploughing day is done; and best of all, sitting by my own fire of a night, with my own people. Because the children are still young there is always so much life in the house, always a sense of chasing and of fast-beating hearts. I love the tumult of it all, feeling myself as a rock in a river. A stepping stone. Nothing gives me more pleasure than to sit at the fireside with one or another of my small ones, Nellie or Jimmy, on my lap; watching the other boys, Mata and Dixie, storm in after some game, famished for a heel of bread and jam and still high to the point of shouting; and if they happen to have along some friend, to see my nine-year-old Annie struck suddenly shy, she just starting to become aware – albeit in the most innocent of ways, yet – of differences worth noticing. And I like, of a morning, listening to our younger girl May as she sings, the words a murmur on her lips but the melody clean as birdsong, always easily recognisable a bar or two along, as 'The Minstrel Boy' maybe, or 'Silver Threads Among the Gold'. I find my faith in these moments, because they are the ones I think of as prayerful.

A little after six, I hear footsteps in the corridor. I am lying on my back on the cell's single cot, and from that position I can see the doorway leaning a couple of black inches ajar. Nobody wants to make this official, so they haven't bothered to lock me in, but it's been made clear that there'll be a charge ready and waiting if I should attempt to step outside without the necessary permission. The bed I have beneath me is like iron, and my mind too restless for the slow thought of sleep, but I move

27

only when the door swings inward at me and Hegarty fills the space, identifiable by nothing other than his shape, until he speaks.

'Jer?' he says, his voice cracking the silence. 'You awake?'

In answer, I sit up, and my bare feet press flat to the floor, relishing the chill punishment of the granite flags. My toes spread themselves, and just for a moment I am overcome with a recollection of playing with Mamie in the Pond Bank, the river that cuts through the centre of the village; I maybe five or six, she that little bit older. Up to our thighs in the cold rushing water, laughing together as we set in place scraps of timber for a blocking, and I doing just this same thing: my toes wallowing in the silt of the riverbed.

'I thought you'd need a cup of tea.' Hegarty steps into the cell, hands me a mug, sits down on the cot beside me, and takes a noisy sip from his own cup. I taste the tea carefully, and find it too sweet for my liking. Still, I am grateful for it, and the sugar cuts away the sour aftertaste of last night's porter. I take a second swallow then cradle the mug for small warmth against my chest.

'We've been over it and back most of the night, and Tom, that is to say, the Sergeant, is of the opinion that we'd be doing you an awful wrong by keeping you from the funeral.'

I look at him. 'You're letting me out?'

'There's a condition. We'll come, too. We're off duty in a couple of hours so we'll be out of uniform, and sure we'd be showing our faces there anyway, as a mark of respect. You can be with your family, and we'll keep well back. But we'll be on hand. We know your word is good, I told you that last night, but grief can do funny things to a man. If anything happens, we can step in.'

For a few seconds the night ahead of dawn seems to deepen, and the weight coming down on my shoulders threatens my balance. I put the mug down beside me on the cot out of fear that it will slip from my fingers to shatter on the cold floor. My sister is dead. My own flesh and blood. I've known a lot of death in my life, but this is different. I have an odd but vivid sense that I am ebbing away. I take another sip of tea, wince at its sweet warmth, and finally clear my throat and thank Hegarty for the consideration.

After I'd come out of the army for the first time, I got home one day from work to find my mother at the table, head bowed in her hands. Mary hovered helplessly alongside, her weight set on one hip, without knowing quite what to say or where to go. When I entered the cottage she started, looked at me in an imploring way and began to cry, too. For a second I thought something had happened to Mata, our infant, and turned cold all over, but then I heard the child murmuring from the cradle beneath the room's small window and released the lump from my throat. I moved through the room in a few quiet strides, and my mother never raised her head, and after just the slightest hesitation I eased past Mary and went out through the back door into the Hall Field, picked open the buttons of my shirt and began to wash myself with cold water from the half-full rain barrel. The day was damp and the oak trees behind our house full of noise in the October breeze, and while Mary, who'd followed me out, watched tearfully, I washed in methodical fashion with a stump of carbolic soap. When I'd rinsed the soap away she handed me a towel and told me why my mother was distressed. Word had come out from town that Michael Egan was dead. That's how she put it, watching me, seeking I suppose some sign that I was about to crumble. *Is he?* was all I said. And, *How did he die?* Wiping the rainwater from my face, feeling my voice tightening but determined not to let my upset show. I hadn't seen or spoken to the old man in the better part of twenty-five years, not since I'd started out of my boyhood and quite a few years yet before I was shipped off to Africa with the Munster Fusiliers. I'd not had word from him in all that time, but I knew from the letters Mamie wrote to me that he'd been in occasional touch with her and, through her, with my mother. Mamie had some need of him and that much I could make sense of, but my mother ought to have steered miles wide of his approaches, given how badly he'd let her down. Yet in some simple, cruel, headlong way, she loved him. The heart wants what it wants, I suppose, and as far as I knew she never again looked at another man. Not that they'd have been lining up for her, and she a woman so far fallen, at least not for anything more serious than a late walk on some lonely road, away from prying eyes. We're all laden with sin, but the shame shows differently on some of us than on others.

Michael Egan wore his sins more discreetly. Or maybe it was that no one cared. Men can get away with things that women can't, and out of sight really is out of mind. And he was able to live almost his entire adult life as a married man, a state of grace, however sullied a one, that would never be afforded my mother. By the time my sister and I were born, he was already wed, to some woman from Glanmire. Or perhaps it was he who'd come from Glanmire, and she was a city girl; I don't quite recall. But either way, married, and I think already a father. I often wondered about his wife – who she was, what she looked like, how they came to be together and whether what she had with him was any kind of love or simply some practical arrangement, he being just someone to set up home with, and to provide while a family was being reared, a body to help her keep loneliness at bay. Was it love, or had he got her in trouble, as he had my mother, with the difference being that this woman had family who urged him to do the right thing by putting the double barrels of a shotgun to the back of his head? It wouldn't have taken much to find out: a few pints in one or two of the right pubs, a bit of chat at the counter until the right names came up. But what good would knowing do? And I learned not to ask my mother too much about him, or about what turns led to Mamie and me, because of the pain such questions caused.

I know he had children with his wife, two boys and two or three girls, though there may of course have been others. Of his legitimate family, the eldest girl was just months older than Mamie, and by the time of Michael Egan's dying – 1910, if I'm remembering right – the youngest boy was only in his mid or late teens. So, brothers and sisters to Mamie and me, clueless as they must have been of our existence and without us knowing much of theirs. I used to wonder if the wife was aware of us, and what she knew of our circumstances, our workhouse start followed by the life we'd had to lead, the struggles and the unending fear of losing whatever ground on normality we'd managed to gain, and I suppose I took it for granted that, since word of her husband's passing had come out to us from the city, she must have known enough.

That night, with the news about Michael Egan still fresh for us, we sat watching the fire, the kindling burning down around clods of turf, and the whimper of my mother's weeping stripped all ease from the evening's stillness. Then, as the hour grew late, she began to sing, something she'd never before done in my hearing, at least not that I could remember. Leaning back from the fire's glow and draped in night, she cleared her throat and built an air that was slow in finding its shape. Long seconds passed before I recognised the lyrics of her song

as Irish, and then I could only bow my head, understanding few of the words, and let myself be taken along
by the lilt of her melody. Mary and I sat shoulder to
shoulder by the fire, her arm tucked inside mine, and
the song that filled the room was a melancholic thing,
like the lament of a gale sifting the crags of a bare hillside.
Minutes then my mother sang, the sense of longing or
grief intensified by such stately cadence, until she slowed
once more and was absorbed back into the silence, leaving
behind only the running hush of her breathing.

'That was beautiful,' Mary said, and she tightened her
grip on my arm when Mata, behind us in his cradle,
stirred and squealed something perfunctory from his
sleep.

'I haven't sung in I don't know how long.' My mother
sounded embarrassed. 'Not in any proper way. And that's
an old one. My own poor mother had such a fondness
for the air. It's odd, isn't it? The things we carry with
us, I mean. Christ above in heaven, is it any wonder I'm
stooped? "*An Droimeann Donn Dílis*". I doubt I've given
that song a thought in fifty years, and I hadn't realised
I still knew it until just now.'

My mother opened up about her life rarely, and never
that I could recall in such a free way as this. As she spoke
I had a sense that she was holding her past close enough
to line up all her dead.

'On Clear Island,' she went on, 'when I was still just
a young one, on winter nights when the weather had us
all inside, we'd press close to whatever kind of a fire was

going. If there was a drop of something to be had in the house, you'd get someone reaching for the fiddle at the least asking, and somebody else would join in on the whistle, and we'd all take turns singing to pass the hours. Either that, or my mother would tell tales fit to put the hair standing on our heads, or she'd recollect monstrous storms that devoured fishing boats and did what they could to beat flat the whole of west Cork, and we'd all delight, us kids especially, in the chill of a terror that we could shiver over without feeling too threatened.'

Mary shifted in her chair. 'So you're a west Cork woman. Did you know that, Jer?'

'I didn't, love.' It hurt me to admit as much. 'Or if I did know, I forgot.'

'West is right,' my mother said, with a lilt in her voice that I recognised from her younger days. 'As west as can be, going back forever. For my mother, and the people gathered by that fire, those nights were about remembering the older ways. No one had anything then, not outside of the few big houses across on the mainland; in the years previous a good number had died among our own crowd, and plenty more gone away, glad of the boat from Cork across to England or America, and I remember that we were all of us still all the time afraid.'

'Can you translate the song for us, Mam? Just to give us a sense of it?'

I was ashamed at having to ask, but Irish for me had all the muffled weight of a foreign tongue, and the only people I knew who kept any of it going were those who'd blown in from the Gaeltacht areas of the countryside or the islands, or who came out of houses under people of such a background, and who still spoke it as a natural inclination. My mother had long since let the language slip from her days, and it existed within her now as an undercurrent, strong and steady but rarely rippling the surface. English had become the language of work and the turning world, and the weapon for keeping hunger at bay.

She took her time in answering. I saw suggestions of her face in the fire's light when she leaned forwards in her chair, and watched as she dragged her mind back from where it had been.

'It's about a good brown cow. Faithful, I suppose, might be the better word. A Droimeann is a native breed of cattle. But I think the song is really about the things we cry for when they're taken from us. And then how we go on from that. That's in the melody if not in the words. And I suppose it's about how we feel when some bit of the past that we thought was gone rises to the surface without us expecting it.'

Even now, sitting and drinking tea with Hegarty, I can feel that earlier night around me just as it was, the sad contentment and the sweet stink of the smouldering turf ashes. My mother hidden by darkness ahead; my baby Mata behind me in his crib, the first of the six children we'd have; and at my side, gripping my hand, Mary, the only woman I've ever wanted. In my mind, I see myself surrounded by my family, because who else looks out for us in the world? And now they are at home, surely wondering where I am and probably terrified over what I might be doing. Locked away on such a morning, I hate myself for the fool I've been in forgetting how much I still have to lose. My anger over poor Mamie's early end has not cooled, and I ache to visit Spillane and drag him out into the road. But settling him now would cost me far too high a price. It'd break down everything I've strived to build.

As soon as it is light outside, Tom Canniffe gives me my coat and leads me to the front door of the barracks. I have the thought that he'll accompany me down to the cottage, but at hardly a hundred yards of a walk, I suppose he feels I can be trusted. A mist has gathered and turned the morning vague, obscuring the road and the ditch opposite. It's not yet eight o'clock and, so far, nothing is stirring.

'Go straight home, Jer,' he says, and despite being sheltered within the doorway he braces himself against the air's bite. 'I'll just get out of the uniform and we'll see you over at the church. Look after yourself now.'

He offers me his hand, and with the slightest hesitation I accept the gesture. Then I flatten my cap down on my head, tug the peak low, and turn away. I walk slowly, in part to spite the early hour's grimness but also because I need the sense of feeling alone. At first I am aware of Tom watching after me from the barracks' doorway, but then the mist closes in around me and we are lost to one another. I draw the cold air and try to resist thought, but Mamie is right there, her face as clear as I've ever known. Eyes glassy, bones pressing against her thin skin, and that way she has of smiling, always slightly awry, as it tends to be with delicate types who move carefully in the world, the dread of so many things having plucked it crooked – whether by a debt that can't be paid, the thought of the children forced to go without, a shouted word when there's been drink involved, or, worst of all, a hand raised not in idle threat but with intent. With the mist making ghosts of everything, she is all I see. And I feel as if I've been scraped hollow.

Mary hurries to me when I enter the cottage but at the last instant pulls back, and we face one another awkwardly in the gloom of our partitioned hallway. When she asks if I'm all right, I nod and tell her that I am, but she considers me anyway, scrutinising me from face to waist and back again, looking for bruises and marks, hints of suffering. She has no fondness for the guards, though she has known Tom Canniffe all her life and thinks him decent enough. It has to do with the uniform, different somehow from that of a soldier's because of the power it wields; but more than that it has to do with the sense of them being always on duty, always watching. To her, guards are men who live in the hope of catching other people's flaws. They'll chat and act easy, but every question has a back to it, and they are never simply themselves.

'I'm fine,' I repeat, and move past her in as gentle a way as I can manage and sit down on one of the chairs by the fire which, despite this early hour, has already flattened from its blaze. The dog Snowy has slipped in through the door behind me and comes to sit at my side. I drop my hand from the armrest and let my fingers scratch at the scruff of his neck and the soft place beneath his ear. I lean back, close my eyes and listen to the old blackened iron kettle on its crook whistling towards an unhurried boiling point. From the bedroom, I catch the small voice of my mother urging the children to get ready, and though the shut door has tamped the sound I can feel she is haggard with grief. When I open my eyes again, Mary has our youngest, Nellie, in her arms, and is perched on the stool opposite, watching me again.

'Nothing happened, love.' The laughter that tinges my words feels uneasy in my mouth and after a beat or two I let it fall away. The baby is quiet but awake, and watchful. I move forwards in my chair and hold out my arms, and Mary, tired also and glad to be for a moment unburdened, passes her to me. 'I had a couple of jars too many in Barrett's and might have run my mouth a bit about Spillane. Drink is liable to do that.'

'I thought you might have gone and done something stupid.'

I shake my head. 'Somebody caught the wrong end of the stick, that's all.'

'Pat Hegarty came down to let me know where you were. He didn't give me the rights of it, except to say

38

that they were keeping on to you, and that they'd have you back to me first thing.'

'I'm sorry about it, Mary. They meant well enough, and in all honesty, the night locked away gave me time to put some things straight in my head. Still, I can't think of Mamie without choking up. She was such a sweet creature.'

'The sweetest.'

'And she'd not an ounce of happiness her whole life, short as it was. Christ, but that fella has a lot to answer for.'

'Don't, Jer,' Mary says. 'Not now. Not today.'

I drink the tea she makes, and without any kind of appetite chew my way through a slice of buttered soda bread. Then I go out into the yard to wash and shave, and afterwards get into the only suit I own, a tired grey double-breasted worsted, the jacket long and loose-fitting on my big frame, that I bought with my leaving money after my first discharge from the army and which I've known hang better on me some years than others. It's the suit I married in, and that I've worn on every significant occasion since, at least on those occasions when the uniform wouldn't do.

The cottage this morning is full but doesn't feel that way. Everyone seems to be making themselves small, and apart from the occasional heave of my mother's wet sighing, the drizzle against the thin panes of the window glass is the front room's dominant sound. After dishing up porridge for the children, Mary hides herself in housework, until my mother gathers the young ones together and announces that they'll all go on ahead, because she has a mind to light a candle and to maybe say a few prayers before the crowd arrives. And as quiet as our home had already been, their leaving brings on a new depth of silence. I hear Mary clearing her throat once, and then she comes through into the bedroom and puts on her good dress, a cotton thing the colour of pepper, a cast-off from one of the houses that she cleans on the Passage Road, and too light for the season. She smooths it into place down the length of her body, as I sit at the end of the bed and run a brush over the scuffed leather of my boots, trying to get a shine on them. Her glance drops onto me, likely snagged by the movement of my hands, but distance holds between us and when she notices me watching she nods her head in a way perceptible only because of how it bothers the shadows across her face. She slips on her navy box coat and presses the pin of the broad belt snugly into its notch, and just as we are about to take the short walk over the lane to the church, she loosens the ribbon in her hair and lets it spill down in a black mess over her upturned collar, in the same way that she sometimes does in bed for me, just ahead of our lovemaking. I watch while she pulls a headscarf from her pocket, a paisley pattern of violet and ivy green, and ties it down across her head, and it is only then, seeing her wrapped so tightly, that I realise how much weight she has lost in the eighteen months since having Nellie. Forty pounds at least, and on a frame that could already scarcely afford the shedding. Outlined by the headscarf, the jut of her chin and spread of her cheekbones mark how sunken her eyes have become, and how hawkish her nose. I know that what I am seeing cannot be good, and though my mind should be on a dozen other things, it's at such moments that the truth often reveals itself. She sees me notice but nothing changes within her demeanour. We're going to have to talk, but tonight, or tomorrow, or next week. Not now. This morning's grief is for Mamie.

Mary runs a hand back over her head to ensure a certain smoothness, then steels herself. I open the door and let her pass me. Her face turns pallid as she steps out into the fog and her shoulders bow against the morning's cold, and it is all I can do not to urge her back inside, to sit a while longer by the fire.

'Come on, Jer,' she says, without turning from our front gate, her voice hushed. 'Let's just get through today. Then we can set ourselves to other worries.'

At the graveside a few people shelter beneath umbrellas, and others huddle together in sullen fashion, faces teeming, caps bunched in tight fists at their sides or hats pressed to their chests in some gesture of penitence or respect. The morning being a Thursday, the church had been three-quarters empty, and felt cold and unwelcoming, but at Mary's insistence we took up places in the front row. I'd wanted to sit near the aisle but Mary had moved me in among the children because Spillane was already sitting on the end of the pew across from us, mindless not only of us but of his own kids, too, and already sweating, even at such an hour and on such a day. What I saw when I glanced at him was somebody numbed by all that had happened, and perhaps guilty for the part he'd played. He sat there, rigid as any of the painted chalk statues of Jesus, Mary and Joseph perched on plinths around the front of the church, in a black suit that was either borrowed from a neighbour or else hired out from the pawn, with a greatcoat draped over the back of his seat and a sodden homburg perched on his lap, and I'd have happily done for him right then, church be damned, but there was something about those staring eyes, so cold and faraway, lost and wide, that caused a shift in me. And all the rage that for the past few days had been cutting me up like an ulcer was doused by a sudden and unanticipated gout of pity. I still hated him enough to want him boiled in tar, but at that moment there could be no denying the sting of compassion in my blood, especially because along from him in his pew, keeping an arm's reach apart from him, were his children, Mamie's children, the only remaining echoes now of who she'd been. The eldest boy, just about to turn thirteen, sitting small but steadfast, marshalling the chasm that had opened up within their family, clinging to that task; the second lad, four years younger, remarkably like his mother in looks and every bit as gentle in his way; and between them the girl, younger still, just five, holding their hands and weeping. What sun there'd been in

Mamie's life had risen and set with these children, and for her memory, and not wanting to increase their suffering, I forced myself to sit quietly through the Mass.

Now, in the cemetery, in the teeming rain and through the last of the prayers, I've made sure to stay back, saving myself the sight of the coffin in its low place, and what I have before me of the grave is a wall of steaming black earth scratched with shovel marks and ribbed with spokes of tree root. And lining the far side, Spillane, already doughy with whatever drink he's taken – just to calm himself, he'd likely explain, were anyone bothered enough to challenge him about it – and now, because of the conditions, turned lumpen; and on his left but again keeping to that step's remove, the children, ordered as they'd been in the church, unnaturally still and well behaved this morning, their faces small and heavy with fatigue. They stare back at me, and I want more than anything to circle the grave and sweep all three of them into my arms, and reassure them that for as long as I am above ground I'll see them all right, because haven't we the same blood in us after all, and don't we share at least part of the same story?

But I can't move, just as there were times in battle when I couldn't, despite the fact that remaining still meant an almost certain end, with bombs tearing open the ground around us in spectacular patterns or the forests on every side ablaze, and the night sky the sickly shade of withered apple skins. All of us who fought suffered these moments, flashes of living death, when the

43

life we had fell into shadow and we got to glimpse a deeper state: heaven, maybe, for some; hell for others; and nothingness for those of us who could no longer believe in either.

The rain keeps up its heavy strum, down among the bones of all who've gone before, and in between flaps of a bleak west wind come snatches of some prayer that the others at the graveside seem to know, their stiff mouths moving to follow its shape. I grit my teeth and think about something I've often heard said, that happy is the corpse the rain falls on, and draw a picture in my mind of Mamie smiling, as she so often had, despite everything. And with that image comes laughter, her laughter, a summer sound from when she and I were children, up the bogs after tadpoles, frogs and ladybirds, or else hunting for a glimpse of the corncrake or the skylark up in the long-grass fields towards Hilltown, because we often wandered miles in those days, starting out at the splitting of the day, she clutching my hand and taking care of me, my big sister, and I having to keep to a little running step to stay at her pace.

Mary leans against me, and I feel her weight, slight enough but so familiar. Around us, an end has been reached. The priest closes his book, slips it back into his pocket and with one black-gloved fist draws the lapels of his coat tightly together beneath his chin. For a few seconds the small crowd retains its stillness, no one wanting to be the first to desert. Then Spillane, straight across from me, turns and starts shaking hands with

44

those standing nearby, and accepting kisses from the women, and whatever trance the prayers might have conjured comes apart and I feel the slam of rage again, because of how he acts as if this is just another day, with the pub waiting and laughter and songs to be had. Beside him, or behind him because of how he has turned away, the children are still and silent, wrapped up in old coats, bare heads hung, eyes bewitched by the depth and finality of the grave, and by the heap of earth at a few paces' remove which within the hour will be bedded back in place, and if Mary hadn't a grip of me, I might well have leapt across the hole between us and killed him. Without giving him time to set himself, I'd have smashed his face with my forehead and either finished him off against the corner of the nearest headstone or else pressed him down in the mud until he stopped kicking. But just as that thought takes on the form of a possibility, Tom Canniffe moves to my side, nodding his sympathies to Mary, reaching for my mother's hand, and touching my right arm just above the elbow, telling me how sorry he is for my trouble, and behind him, across the grave, I see that my kids are with their cousins, with May trying to get them all under an umbrella that somebody has given her, and Annie with her arm around William trying to comfort him while he stands, shoulders shaking.

Through most of our childhood, Mamie used to tell people that our father was dead, that he'd been a soldier killed in Africa. She'd concocted an entire fable, and would deliver it with authority and conviction whenever the subject was raised, in a way that made her easier to believe than to doubt, talking about how after the regiment had been ambushed in a narrow valley and mostly slaughtered, he and his few remaining comrades had managed to escape and take shelter in a small shed. There they resisted for a full day and night despite being outnumbered more than a thousand to one, because the Zulus, with their incessant battle cries curdling the prairie darkness, were armed with nothing more than spears and knives and had no chance against the British Army rifles. But when the ammunition ran out, early on the second morning, the place was quickly overrun. Some of the men were hacked to pieces with machetes and fed to the lions. Our father, she told anyone who'd listen, had continued to fight, armed only with his bayonet, for a long time after all the others had fallen, until an unlucky spear caught him in the chest and pinned him to the trunk of the ancient thorn tree that he'd been using to protect against rear attacks. Because the Zulus so respected his bravery they waited a full hour more before approaching his body, though it must have been obvious to all that he was dead, sending the dogs in first and only then closing around him, arms at the ready and with the greatest of caution. They left his carcass pinned to the tree for the wild animals to eat but cut off his head, the highest honour they could bestow on an enemy, she said – talking of things she couldn't possibly have known even if a single word of it had been true – and kept it as

46

a prized trophy mounted on a spike at the entrance to their village, believing it would intimidate neighbouring tribes and ward off evil spirits. If our mother was within earshot, in the doorway of the terrace in Bog View, maybe chatting with one or two of the neighbouring women or just taking a few minutes of air away from her chores, she'd look on, her expression knotted into a tight silence, and though we'd sometimes hear her clearing the catch in her throat she never made any effort to contradict her daughter with the actual facts.

I knew, of course, that Mamie was spinning a yarn, but there were times, listening to her, when I yearned for what she was saying to be true and when I wanted more than anything to be able to swallow her words the way some of the other kids did. The tale was attractive, the goriness and glory of it as well as the idea that I could possibly have come from such brave and heroic soldierly stock, but it took me a bit longer to realise that, for her, talking like this was a way of shielding us, all three of us, my mother, too, from what others must have been thinking and saying. She and I were born barely a mile from Douglas, but we arrived into the village as strangers, the three of us reddened clean from the delousing and carbolic scrubbing that they'd put us through in the workhouse ahead of our discharge, and with the truth of our situation hinted at by our bare feet and the clothes that pooled around us, waiting to be grown into. How we survived, I can't begin to know, except to say that we wouldn't have had our mother been anything other than who she was, a gentle soul with us but a wild animal against any kind of threat, and willing to sacrifice everything of herself for our well-being. As young as I was when we left the workhouse, the memory of it is locked within me, with its huge high-ceilinged dormitories, cobbled yards and uniformed guards defined by their watchful stillness and the truncheons they carried in their fat hands. And I remember the fear, and the awful sounds of people crying out in the night, from despair and maybe for other more specific reasons, too. But these are fragments that my mind has saved, with the fogged sensations and texture of dreams, so that I'm not always sure if I have recalled actual moments or concocted them. And from hearing men who'd been to war with me speak of workhouses and other institutions of the kind, either at home or in England, I count myself fortunate not to have preserved more of my time within its walls.

On arriving in Douglas we sheltered in the small house in Bog View, and for the first couple of years occupied a corner of one room, with our bed a nest of sacking that smelled sweet when we curled up together at night, Mamie folding me into a tight embrace and our mother, at our backs with her arms around us both, calming us with sounds that didn't seem like words at all, her mouth beside my ear so as not to disturb the rest of the house. I remember too, from our doorway of a cold night, watching the stars spilling away westwards in uncountable numbers over Vernon Mount and its woods and bogs, trying to make shapes out of the dust-spays of light and wondering what they were and why they were there and how they kept themselves from falling. That, and eating without sitting down, and playing games of it with Mamie, making each bite of the watery porridge first something rich and delicious: goose, buttered turnips, carrots, apple cake, chocolate; and then, amid disgusted peals of laughter, something entirely foul: dog shit, pieces of rat, a gob of phlegm, an eyeball, I pulling increasingly revolted faces at her ever-worsening suggestions and, with the best ones, adding the exaggerated action of a dry, reaching heave. And I also remember being often afraid, especially at night, lying there with straw digging into my flesh and the itch of the nibbling fleas, my mind tuned to lurking sounds and thinking about what we had and what, for us, was missing. The people around us had little more to their name than we had, but that little, earned by the man of the house from long shifts in one or another of the village's mills, made all the difference and secured for them the kind of existence that we could never quite count on. More than steady work, though, what gave them all the higher ground was their lack of shame. With established marriages and children rightfully named, they could walk into the church or schoolhouse and not hesitate to look people in the eye. They met us with hesitance, the sight of a still-young mother without a seed of a husband to be found telling our tale well enough, but since everyone had it all to do in dealing with their own problems it was easier for them not to look too closely into who we really were. The excuse our mother gave about her man being a soldier killed in fighting was nodded at and shrugged away. And if some of the neighbouring women were initially grudging with their friendliness, not yet sure what they had in front of them and maybe not trusting their own husbands to behave as gentlemen, then they were still kind enough in their ways, especially to Mamie and me.

Mamie's narrative expanded on our mother's, adding colour and infusing it with such drama that it soon became something others enjoyed hearing. She was running a risk with specifics, especially in front of those men who'd actually soldiered abroad, in India or Africa, and who surely could have spoken up if they'd so desired. But I suppose having seen as much as they had of the world, and having known far worse sins than fatherless children, they likely understood what she was doing, and why.

If Mamie's yarns protected her, I defended myself in other ways. From a young age I could fight, and in school, right from the beginning, I had no hesitation in facing up to the other boys for remarks they passed. I'd meet them over between the Catholic and Protestant graveyards, where it was almost always quiet, and I'd take off my tunic and have at it with them, filling up their mocking grins with blood, blackening their eyes and getting their noses going, not letting up even on the few occasions when it looked as if they'd taken some serious hurt, my small fists always ready to swing. When

I fought I made no concession and gave no thought to consequences; I simply wanted my opponent gone, wiped out. This made me dangerous, and those who'd gathered to watch often had to step in and press me flat to the ground until my madness passed. Someone always told, or talked when questioned about the damage done and who it was that caused it, and I was usually hauled up before the teacher. If I hadn't gone too far the price was a smashing, the willow switch numbing my fingertips, but if I had they'd draw welts across my ass and the backs of my legs, of such stinging intensity that I'd weep for days afterwards at having to sit. I didn't always win my fights, but on those occasions when I'd crossed someone from the older classes and got knocked to pulp I still put a bit of fright into them, and into those looking on, too, the girls and boys alike, by continuing to get to my feet even when I could only remain upright with the help of something solid to brace against. Finishing what their words had started proved too much for most stomachs, and finally even the toughest boys turned away, laughing to conceal their failure, and after that they tended to be careful with the things they said. The worst of the fighting rage had passed from me by the time I'd entered my teens, but I could afford by then to be friendly, knowing that the kids in and around the village would either remember or have heard enough not to want to take me on.

Against all of this, Michael Egan was a ghost. Never there, and not much more to us than a name, but always somehow looming. The first time I mentioned him to my mother she cried. I couldn't have been more than four or five, and all I'd done was ask what he was like, and why he didn't live with us, but because it was obvious that I'd hurt her deeply I ran outside and followed the river up into the bogs, until I reached a spot where the slow run of the water below me lost its sound. I remained a long time in the high grass, and only started back for home once the July light turned heavy just ahead of night. Back in the house nobody said anything, and Mamie looked at me in a disappointed way and shook her head, as if I ought to have known better, and after that night I only ever mentioned Michael Egan when my mother happened to bring him into the conversation – 'Your father had a coat just like that' or 'You walk just like him, Jer, with that bit of a sway you have'. If I caught her in the right mood she'd sometimes give a little, mentioning that he had worked for most of his life as a gardener, but fell back when he had to on whatever work was going, running dogsbody chores, digging roads, and scrubbing and lime-washing walls. Or that it was after his father that I'd been named, Jeremiah Egan, that old man a farm labourer the last she'd heard but a soldier in his younger days, twenty years with the King's Rifles, stationed much of that time in the West Indies. I was greedy for such details, but because with my mother, at least on this subject, the weather could change in half a heartbeat, I sat tight, straining to listen but letting her set the speed.

Later on, Mamie and I were taken for the first time to meet him, and over the few years that followed we saw and got to know him a little bit for ourselves, though only as much as he wanted known. I can't say what prompted the visits, which never occurred more than once or twice in the year and always on the terms that he dictated, of a Saturday or, more usually, of a Sunday. I recall being decked out in the best of what little good clothes I had going, in the front room of one of the houses off Barrack Hill which wasn't his and, I later learned, had been borrowed for the hour, either as a favour or for money; and my abiding memory is of keeping perfectly still in the middle of the floor and staring up at the man looming above me, a figure so towering against the blanched backdrop that I needed to squeeze my eyes a little in order to see, and had to sift through the shadows of his face to find him.

Because of how they were rationed, each meeting was a thrill but also more than a little traumatic, since Mamie and I were never prepared or forewarned. We'd simply be taken on the tram, thinking it was just another trip into town: down along the Coal Quay to the cluttered street stalls if our mother needed elastic for her stockings or thread for darning, or into the great brick enclosure of the English Market at the city's heart, for crubeens or tripe or pig skirts or a piece of smoked coley, whatever could be got for a pittance that day and made to feed three, all the while staring agog at the big wide chaos of the place with its bustling throngs of shawled women, the brackish air around us damp from sea and river drifts. Usually, Michael Egan insisted on seeing us one at a time, as if having to bear both of us at once would have been overwhelming, and the way I remember it, he had Mamie in more often than he would me, maybe feeling that she needed it more, she being of an age to better understand, but also because he had a fondness for her that we could all see, though we knew better than to speak of it. It made me sad to think I was less important to him, but I put the fighting part of myself to such a thought and tried not to let it matter. And despite my hurt I was glad to see how being singled out in such a way made Mamie feel about herself, how it kept her smiling for days at a time, though it always unsettled her once the shine of the visit had worn off, and on many of those aftermath nights I was the one who hugged her and kissed her cheeks while she cried herself to sleep.

For us, young as we were and confused by the whole business, the encounters felt at the same time real and fantastic, because when we later questioned one another in an attempt to share whatever it was that we'd experienced, the scene often failed to line up with our expectations. After one such visit, I might have reported him as tall, thin and pallid; Mamie, having perhaps met him while he was sitting, found him squat and big-shouldered, with worried eyes. To her his voice was always tight, close to a dog's growl, while with me his talk was almost entirely breath. She and I could discuss him for hours and still somehow manage to skirt the facts of who he actually was, and he proved an easy and natural topic because we built him into an almost mythical figure, of the sort who loses all distinction as soon as he has stepped out of sight. As I've said, a ghost.

After Mamie's funeral, late into the night I lie with my wife in our narrow bed, turned to one another as we often are when sleep refuses us, pressed together with our faces inches apart. I have the window at my back, and through the blanket can feel a draught from where the putty has worn to dust along the lowest part of the frame.

'He's taking them away,' Mary says.

There is almost no sound to her words, but this is a method of communication that we've mastered through practice, speaking largely in shapes, answering in felt nods and weighted breaths, the way lovers have to when a room is shared with others apart from themselves.

'What? Who's taking who away?'

'Spillane. The kids. They're going to England. A place called Rochdale. That's in Lancashire, somewhere up near Manchester.'

'I know Lancashire. I know where Rochdale is. He can't do that, can he?'

'They're his kids. He's entitled.'

'I'll talk to him.' I make to sit up but her hand falls across me and I yield. 'He's panicking, that's all. I've no fondness for the man but this has to have hit him hard. I'll go and see him, let him know we're here to help out.

Leaving would be a desperate wrench for the children.'
My mind feels heavy. I close my eyes, then open them
again. 'What's dragging him up to Rochdale, anyway?
Relatives, is it?'

'A sister. Margaret. She went across to London early
on, to work in one of the hospitals. And at some point
I suppose she married and moved north. The husband
is on the railway and can sort Spillane with work. And
they've found him a place to rent, the upstairs of a house
near their own.'

I listen, but the pieces won't seem to fit together. All
I can see are problems.

'How do you know so much, love?'

She hesitates. 'Your mother told me.'

Her breathing taps against my chin and cheek, and
there is a hint of sour milk about her mouth, as if she's
been recently sick; not an overwhelming smell but
unpleasant enough that it should make me want to turn
my face away. Yet it's something I've apparently grown
used to, it having become such a quiet permanence in
recent months, and so much a part of who Mary is now
that rather than wanting to pull back I feel a yearning
to pull her closer. It might be a cause for worry, but it
seems that we've chosen not to face these facts until we
absolutely have to.

'Jer?'

'Yes, love?'

'She's going with them.'

'Who is? Mam?'

The pillow shifts a little now with the movement of her head. 'She feels she has no choice, especially if he's going to be working. The children need rearing, and they're Mamie's flesh and blood. Who else can look after them now?'

In this bed, with all the grief there is, we become somehow young again, and small beneath greater things. She moves against me when I bring my mouth to hers, and when I open my eyes I find her gaze waiting, so close that I can feel the tickle of her lashes against my own. In those seconds the familiar quiet frenzy builds and overtakes us, and she helps me lift up the hem of her nightgown and I roll her onto her back and let her shift beneath me.

Afterwards, I get up as softly as I can and slip outside into the yard, to piss. The rain has eased and a mist trawls the night once more in forlorn sheets, and I fill the frame of the back door. To keep herself from calling out, Mary had taken a fold of blanket between her teeth and bitten down into the coarse wool. I'd stayed with her, feeling her gasp as some noise inside her caught and stuttered away in a wet breath against my throat. Her arms and calves had crossed around me, and I'd kissed the hot sourness of her mouth, and when I lifted myself she'd looked up and urged me on, telling me things in some silent way until it was no longer possible to keep anything back, and for the few seconds that followed there was nothing else for us both that mattered.

Knowing that I won't easily sleep, I remain a while in the solitude of the yard until the cold drives me back inside. Not wanting to disturb the others, I take up the armchair in the living room, reach for the poker and stir awake the fire's embers. An orange glow rises up from the feathers of ash, and I add a clod of turf and a few scraps of kindling.

Everything is changing. Until a few days ago, I had a sister. Struggling, and in poor health, but there to visit, to sit with and talk to, she taking my hand whenever she could and mostly ignoring my questions about how she was feeling, to ask instead if I was happy, if I'd gotten what I wanted from my life and if what I had been given was enough, as if I'd had any kind of choice in the way things worked out, as if any of us did. Asking, too, if the war was at all as bad as she felt certain it must have been, if the damage that showed itself on some men, that sort of cracked, glass-eyed madness, was with everyone who'd been through the fighting, even those who had found ways of keeping it concealed. And asking, in the quietest possible way, shyly or with embarrassment, if I ever got lonesome; needing something from me, I sensed, some few words that might begin to explain her own state. In such moments, she couldn't bring herself to look at me and seemed always on the verge of tears, and all I could do was squeeze her cold hands and try to make less of such talk, mainly because I had no good words to give back in response. And now, watching the fire and thinking about all that I've been given and all I've missed out on, I realise that my life is defined every bit as much by absences as by acts. As much as I might think I've suffered, I am finding out there's always something more that can be taken. A few days ago I had a sister, and now I don't. Tonight I have a mother, but a week from now she too will be gone from my life, dealing with Spillane far away from where I can offer any kind of protection. She hasn't lived a day of her adult life for herself, and now that she's found a new need for sacrifice, my attempts to change her mind or Spillane's will be a wasted effort. So he'll go, taking his and Mamie's children with him, and my mother will go too, putting up with whatever it takes to see them reared. Our family might have come up crooked, but she is determined to keep it nourished, and to give it every possible chance to thrive.

I close my eyes and try to concentrate on savouring the wash of the fire's heat across my skin. In France, I recall our commanding officer telling us that indulging too much in memories was precisely the medicine for getting a man killed. And what applied then still hasn't shifted, a fact as true of the most ordinary day as of the bloodiest battle: what's needed to get through it is a focused mind. So now, though I let the thoughts of Mamie come, I am careful to keep them at a step's remove. That's cold of me, because if ever there could be a time and place to open up my heart then it's here and now, alone as I am, by the fire with a high wall of night before me, and with my family, everyone in the world who has my love, safely tucked up and sleeping under this same roof. And yet I can't let myself go, and the only reason I can muster is the fear that if I did, I might never again regain my balance. I visualise Mamie as she'd been last week, pale and worn out from a fortnight of coughing, slight as a fist of straw having shed what little weight she'd previously been carrying. And when those thoughts hurt too much I reach for memories of how she was in her brighter days, beautiful that first or second year of marriage, before drink took a determined grip of Spillane and set about making ruins of them both; and how she'd been as a girl, during all the time we spent together after our mother had found steady work, when for long hours the world was nothing and no one else but us. Running and playing by day, and at night curled up together on our sacking mattress, tucked beneath our mother's old overcoat and listening to the mice in the ceiling, the two of us sharing secrets that could never be otherwise told. The images are there but I keep them to a projection, like pictures spread across a screen, separate from me. I need to be able to put them aside and walk on from them. A certain distance deep into war, the realisation dawns on a man that all there truly is, day after day, is keeping on: facing the fight when it's brought to you but always forging ahead. Results, wins and losses, are for the politicians. For the soldier on the battlefield what counts is not dying.

A week from now this cottage is sure to be a different place. It's people that make a home. We'll miss my mother terribly, and she will ache just as much for us, each one of us in a different way, down to Nellie, our youngest, our baby. And we'll tell ourselves and one another, aloud and in our heads, that England is not the end of the earth, that Lancashire is just a short boat ride across to Dublin and a few hours on the train back to Cork. She can be home in a day and a night, if needs be. We'll say that and try to believe it, but we'll also know, without having to hear it spoken of, that she's already old, and we could very well have seen one another for the last time.

I wake to a hand on my shoulder. I am shivering, my heart slamming with the remnants of a nightmare that has put me in a grey field like those I'd found in Flanders, earth coating my uniform and filling my mouth and nostrils with a bitter rust. It had been silent there, with the cracking of gunfire having spent itself, and the quiet was worse somehow than the noise, like a stuck breath, or like being blind and a step away from the brink. I rub my eyes with the heels of my palms, look up and find Mary, leaning in, her expression concerned for me, her eyes wide and her mouth a small hole around a word I've missed.

'You're cold,' she says again, and I look at her hand, fingers splayed against my shoulder. 'How long have you been sitting here?'

I can't answer because I don't know. I glance at the fire and see that the last embers have lost their glow. I shift in the chair, and Mary takes her hand back.

'You're all right, aren't you, Jer? I mean, you'd say if you weren't.'

'I am,' I tell her, feeling my voice small, but I can see by the way she is watching me that she's not convinced. 'I would. Of course I would, love. I'm just a bit sad, that's all.'

'Well,' she says, deciding with reluctance to accept that, 'go and put something on. The last thing we need now is you getting sick.'

'What time is it?'

'I don't know. Early. Not yet six. Go easy so that you don't disturb the rest of them. We won't get an ounce of peace, otherwise. And we can't expect them to sit still and quiet two days in a row. I'll stir the fire. Then we can talk.'

The cold is everywhere and the air seems to swirl around me. I am still shaking, like in the trenches, except that it's also nothing like the trenches. The house is peaceful, and I have Mary. She hasn't moved, and I feel as if she is seeing inside me, reading me, and there's not a thought in my mind that I begrudge her. Then, as I get to my feet, she steps close and I put my arms around her. Her tears make no sound, and don't touch the cadence of her breathing, but once I've realised they are falling I can feel the quiet pump of her sadness echoing through her body. I tell her that while she has me we'll be fine and will get through whatever comes, kissing her as I talk, her forehead and cheeks and shut eyes, and she turns her face upwards so that I can find her mouth and tries, as she always does, to be strong, knowing I mean everything I say but understanding too that it might not be enough.

II

Nancy

(1911)

Not long ago, my daughter-in-law Mary asked what life had been like for me growing up. We'd had a warm day and were out in the Hall Field in search of a cooling breeze, with the infants, Mata and Annie, crawling in the grass, and because she'd been casual in her asking, I kept my response equally so. But the truth is that I couldn't answer, not in any proper way. The scale of the question overwhelmed me, and in the down moments of all the days and nights since, I've thought of little else, hoping to make sense of it. My life feels like a trail of footprints in a snow-covered field, with a lot of detail obscured. Only the best and worst moments have survived, those that impacted most heavily. During the living of it there was neither time nor room for contemplation – simply surviving took everything I had, and then keeping my little ones alive, safe and fed. If I'd known at the low points along the way how much worse my situation could still get, I do wonder if I might have simply given up, the way plenty did, folks I grew up around or heard about who, deciding they could take no more, hung themselves with a piece of rigging rope from a roof beam, or dug open the wrists of both hands and fell down in the corner of some field to bleed themselves dry, or who stripped down to their skins on one of Clear Island's beautiful sandy beaches and waded out into the sea until the waves submerged them. Because as terrible as any of those choices would have been, as sinful to a soul, according to the priests, they'd have been easier than what followed for me, and who's to say that, when all is said and done, easier isn't better? From inside the living moments, though, grief-stricken as they were and so full of hunger, and as shameful as they'd become once my destitution took full hold, such escapes were beyond consideration. All that mattered was getting by, at any cost.

Our island, ten miles or so west of the mainland, did suffer badly when the hunger hit, or when storms rolled in, but if heaven does exist and has a landscape half as breathtaking as Clear's, especially of a summer's day when the sea is calm and brightly lit and there's not a murmur of wind to freshen the heavy air, then nobody will be disappointed. Patchworked in rough gorse, loose rock walls and winding byroads, Clear is cruel in its beauty, especially along the wild western fringes, a nightmare for boats to navigate even when the weather is at ease, and a place that speaks in ancient ways. Pirates passed winters here, tucked into safe harbour, knowing they were out of reach of the chasing law. And the Spanish, having tamed and terrorised half the world but driven close to our shore by sweeping gales, wrecked the best of their Armada on the treacherous hidden reefs. Sometimes the fog gathers over the land and nearer reaches of sea with such density, a kind of fairy cloak, that anyone standing beyond an arm's reach becomes an island in and of themselves, and if you don't know the ground beneath your feet, it is easy to simply step out into nothingness and be forever lost. There's magic on Clear, of a kind that is just as often wicked as it is good.

I haven't much of a head for dates but I do know that a few days ahead of my birth, in April of '52, my aunt Hannah died, the last of my mother's people to go. Hannah left behind a husband, John Joe, and I heard often from my mother that for days and nights after her death he'd wept like Noah's rain. By that time, other families had begun burning their bodies rather than burying them, partly due to a shortage of priests in the area and partly because the will for dealing in more correct fashion with the dead had long since been crushed, but John Joe insisted on Hannah going into the ground so that she might rest in soil that knew her. Weak as he was from starvation, he spent hours opening the grave of our people, and though there was little my mother could do to help, given her heavily pregnant condition, she remained at the graveside the whole day long and watched him work, and in this way neither of them had to feel alone.

Through the entire dig John Joe didn't utter a word, and he hardly stopped, except once to roll up his sleeves and then again, an hour or so later, to peel off his shirt. In the first onset of dusk, bare-chested and emaciated, he looked like something that had risen up from the earth. The sight had my mother pulling her old shawl tightly across her swollen front, knowing that, stripped down, she'd have looked no better, for the hunger that hacked at the others had ravaged her, too. Once the cloud-smothered light began to wane, she twisted a rag around a stout blackthorn stem in a rough effort at a torch, and set it to burning with some tinder and a piece of flint, so that she could guide him in seeing all the corners of his task. Perched on her knees at the side of the deepening pit, she gripped the stem of the torch with both hands for as long as the rag remained aflame. When finally John Joe got the ground levelled out to a satisfactory depth, too weary either to keep going or to climb out, he simply lay down there and within seconds was asleep. The torch then burned out, and in the absolute blackness my mother stretched herself out an arm's reach from the grave, bedding down on the grass, and tried to remember a time when all the people she'd ever loved were still going, still alive and happy.

In time gone by, because of a belief that the dead and the unborn shouldn't mix – a rule going back as far as memory stretched, and one as trusted on the island as any commandment by any god – she'd have been forbidden entry to a graveyard in her condition. But in those past few years their whole existence had become a graveyard, and all such boundaries were lost. That night my mother waited, with no way of separating wakefulness from sleep, until at last, away to the east, a pale gleam cracked the lowest part of the sky. She struggled to sit up then, and watched the light come again and spread out across the horizon. Despite everything, the day was as alive with promise as a song she couldn't quite hear yet but wanted to, more than anything. And it was at that precise moment, or so she liked to claim, that I stirred inside her, for the first time in weeks. I'd been still for so long that she was full of fear for me, and at my sudden kicking she laid her face into the dirty cradle of her hands and wept. Six days later, not half a mile from that very spot, in the small house that gave us shelter and that we and a long line of those who'd come before us called home, I arrived into the world.

I have known happiness, because a life is never just one thing, and while it might not amount to much when my time is considered as a whole, it remains significant for me. Romance excited my young days in a way that made them seem so much better than they were, a hot burning sun that flared for a brief while, to an intensity that left me forever scorched. That it wasn't both-sided, that what I'd felt hadn't been necessarily returned, hurts, but time's passing has made me realise that it was in no way less real for its shortfalls. And I live now for my children, because when I had nothing I had them, and I knew that

71

I was all they had. To have lasted into old age makes me feel at times as if death has forgotten me, as if I'll be the one to somehow beat the trick. If that sounds like a blessing, it's not. I'm tired, have been for years, but lately I feel spent. I get up in the mornings still wanting sleep and I lie awake deep into the night trying to ignore all the things that have remained at bay during daytime hours, but which come at me once the house has turned quiet. Will the grave be any different? Maybe that's the hell priests talk so much about. Hell might be the ceaseless repetition of who we are during our lowest moments, with our mistakes, the ones that have defined our lives, playing over and over to goad us for all eternity. But I hold on to the consolation that whether heaven or hell awaits me at least I'll be lying down for it. Like I've said, I'm tired.

I was nineteen when I met Michael Egan for the first time. That's not where my story begins, but it's where I begin, that day the beginning of my happiness and the start of my fall. Every significant moment of my life is a page in a pile that a hundred or a thousand years from now can be tossed in the air and recounted from at random as they fall. I am the picture, in any order. But Michael Egan, whether absent or otherwise, is the consistency that gives me shape.

At that age, nineteen, in terms of years still just a girl, I was the last one of my family still living. I'd left Clear Island for the mainland and found a situation in one of the big houses out past Blackpool village on the northside of Cork city, cleaning for and attending to a Mrs McKechnie. A dour Scottish woman mired in late-middle age, she'd been to all intents and purposes abandoned by her husband when, after serving a stint with the 93rd Foot, fighting in the Crimea, at the Siege of Sevastopol, distinguishing himself to the point of medal recognition in some of that campaign's heaviest hand-to-hand combat, he'd taken on a naval commission rather than returning home, and at this point, ten or twelve years in, had risen to the rank of Frigate Lieutenant. Mrs McKechnie was demanding to work for, and had a savage temper, using the smallest excuse to rant at me whenever we were in the same room and begrudging me the three or four hours of sleep that I'd collapse into, somewhere in the early hours, ahead of my regular pre-dawn start. But though she had me in frequent tears with some of the more wicked things she said, it was clear that a lot of her rage and bitterness was misdirected and that I was simply the easiest and most readily available target. And given what I'd already been through in my life, any work that put a bite of food my way and kept some kind of a roof above my head could not be undervalued. Of the five children she'd borne, four boys and a girl, none had made it past infancy, but each had left a distinct and everlasting impression on her, a despair as obvious as any bruise or birthmark; and apart from me and Elizabeth, the cook, an impossibly old woman with hands so arthritic she struggled with the simplest of tasks, the house was empty, all ten bedrooms of it, and our lady would spend the long hours of the day, and often late into the night too, with a stub of candle set in the centre of a saucer, drifting from room to room, sitting a while on one of the chairs, settees or bed-corners, lingering in doorways and keeping up the sort of sighing, one-sided conversations that let her mind feel fully involved but which passed me by in terms of their meaning, and often put chills right through me, sensing that she was seeing ghosts all around us, a fact no less disturbing in daylight than in darkness.

Michael Egan showed up on the Tuesday of my third week. He was tall, a full head above me, with a frame as lithesome as a willow switch and the narrowest shoulders I'd ever seen on a man. When I happened to glance out of the small scullery window and saw him in the back garden, contemplating the flower bed with its small blooms of primroses and pansies and its earth in need of turning, leaning on his shovel, the heel of a hobnailed boot pressing the tip of the blade down into the soil, I felt something give inside myself. I'd known my share of boys and young men from the barn dances down west and had allowed kisses – though nothing more – to be stolen from me by the good-looking few among them, usually on the slow walk home after we'd spun ourselves into a frenzy, so I had a reasonable knowledge of what men were like and how they could make a girl feel, if she let them or if she gave a little of herself over to that. But I was also young enough yet to have my head turned by a fine face and to keep room in my heart for the notion of love; and that morning, through glass that I'd only a couple of days earlier soaped and scrubbed, I couldn't stop staring at how handsome he was. Thinner, yes, than I'd have ideally liked but in that iron way of those who never cower and who'll never go hungry, and I felt drawn to the dangerous ease of his demeanour, an indolence self-assured to the point of cocky, as if space existed entirely for him to fill.

Just the sight of him was enough to unnerve me. The feeling I recall is of my heart sinking down through me, leaving me numb and without air. When he turned, maybe feeling himself being watched, what he'd have seen in the window was a small staring face, skin pale as the innards of a nut, eyes like lumps of anthracite, and equally black feathers of hair, still growing out from a tight cropping because I'd caught lice on my journey in from the west. He'd have noticed the fear in my expression, and the vulnerability, but maybe also some trace of the yearning of someone who'd been for too long without real human connection, and something within all of that was the reason why, after just the briefest hesitation, he cracked a smile. And when, on towards noon, he came knocking on the back door and propped himself with one elbow against the jamb to beg a mug of buttermilk, preferably with a drop of something strong running through it, his grin spelt all manner of trouble, and I felt myself overcome with such weakness in my legs that I had to stop what I was doing, scraping carrots for the night's dinner, and set my hip against the table for support. In the previous few hours when I'd been able to get to a window in between running one chore and another – sweeping the hallway or landing, freshening the beds of the extra rooms even though they weren't going to be slept in, changing the water in the flower vases – I'd seen that he had stripped to the waist for tending to the garden, it being one of those hot May mornings which can easily overpower you if you don't pace yourself with it. And though he had pulled on his shirt again before coming up to the house he hadn't bothered doing up the buttons, and so it hung open, exposing a wide stripe of his body from his throat to the tarnished tin buckle of the belt keeping up his trousers. I considered how his ribs dimpled the flesh of his midriff, and how hair the colour of honey nested like cobweb around the nipple that had nudged into view as he stretched an arm out to lean against the wall. I had never seen a man before in so close and exposed a way, and my gaze refused to yield. He watched me, grinning all the while but saying nothing, letting me fill myself up on the sight of him and relaxing into it, and if there was anything threatening for me about his presence then, it had to do with what I was finding within myself ahead of any danger he posed – though I had no doubt at all, given his comfort in flaunting himself before me, that he was capable of plenty. And once I realised the risk I was running, being so close to a bare-chested man in full view of whoever should walk into the kitchen, I looked away quickly. To be caught flirting, even innocently, would as likely as not cost me my job, and without the security of my work I'd have been a boat adrift among rocks in a strong wind. The table kept me upright and after a few seconds I was able to regain my composure. But it was only when I distracted myself by taking up the jug of buttermilk, pulling away its muslin covering and filling a tall mug almost to the brim, that I could properly breathe again.

He came and looked after the grounds twice a month. The second morning I saw him, he explained that the garden, being the size that it was, with not more than half an acre planted, couldn't justify any more attention paid to it. That second day, knowing he was due back at the house, I had scheduled my work so that I could be outside in the yard when he appeared, hanging out the bedsheets and curtains that I'd laundered the afternoon before, and the clothes lines provided cover for a few minutes of snatched conversation, nothing too improper but with more hinted, and if I blushed at the way he looked at me, wide-openly considering me from head to foot and slowly back again, then I laughed too, with embarrassment and delight, when he told me how fine I was to his eye, a grand bit of stuff despite the lack of meat on my carcass, how he hadn't in an age or for fifty miles seen a smile as pretty as mine and that he'd lie down in his grave a contented man if he was ever to get within a breath of one of my kisses. When he made to grab me I slapped his arm, but playfully, to chase away his grin rather than in outright dismissal, and that same morning, while I was passing through the kitchen, he came to the back door again, not to talk this time or to ask for anything but, because I'd neglected to tell him that I couldn't read, to press a piece of paper into my hand, a note he'd taken the time to scribble. I'd mentioned while in the yard, maybe not as casually as it might have sounded, that unless Mrs McKechnie was entertaining guests, I was generally permitted Sunday afternoons off, though I had to be back in by eight in order to prepare the lady's bath and to heat the irons for warming her bed. After clearing the table following lunch and attending to the washing-up, I usually had the better part of three or four hours free, to go for a walk if the day was fine or to sit in my room or out in the garden and rest, maybe over a bit of stitching, making the most of the chance, with the daylight, to tuck a hem or mend a seam that had worn itself loose. Those few hours counted as my day of rest, and I was glad of them, and Michael Egan, still grinning, nodded and said that, with the world the way it was, we needed indeed to make the most of whatever few hours were given to us.

That afternoon, as soon as I could, I slipped into the kitchen where Elizabeth was stirring soup from the vegetables that I'd earlier chopped and washed for her. She stared at me when I took the note from my apron and asked if she'd read it, but then wiped her hands on a cloth, cleared her throat and in a voice pitched low against being overheard, delivered the loosely lettered request that I meet him at the bottom of Spangle Hill the very next bit of time I had off so that we might spend our Sunday afternoon together. Just hearing the words filled me with excitement and apprehension and set my blood to prickling.

Though I was just nineteen, I didn't at the time feel young. Years of malnourishment had scuffed whatever beauty I might have once possessed. I'd survived ahead of plenty who'd been stronger than me, my father and mother, and neighbours and other islanders too, but was nonetheless reduced to sackings of skin. Washing before bed, stooping above an old porcelain basin of tepid water, pummelled from the day's work and so weary in every muscle that even breathing took chunks from me, there were nights when I wept at the sight of my naked self in the tallow candlelight, ribs showing through the skin like the spindly branches of a birch in winter, and the sag of my poor pathetic breasts, wasted and shrunken before they'd had the chance to properly sprout and hanging flat to my body, the sight of me not at all the way a woman was supposed to look. And then came Michael Egan, and his note.

I showed little enthusiasm over the request, because innocent as I was with regard to such matters I still knew well enough what he was chasing, and that any kind of keenness on my part would have been quickly and eagerly misconstrued. Yet neither could I bring myself to be outright with a refusal, believing I had little about me that might ever again attract the attentions of another man. Instead of responding, I kept busy enough through the rest of the afternoon that our paths hadn't needed to cross, but in the days after, as I lay awake in my small bed, waiting for the workday to begin, I dared wish that his interest might really lead to something good and true, that he, like any man, needed a woman to set up home with, to bear and bring up a family and to split the burden of daily living, and while there were plenty of reasons why that woman should not have been me it did seem, if the note stood for what I hoped it did, that I might be the one he'd choose. Michael Egan may have been a long fall short of perfect, arrogant in a way that wasn't half earned and the type seemingly far too relaxed with the single life, but I knew from what I'd seen of him in the garden that he could work when he wanted to, that he was at least strong and able, and lying with him in the night had to be a sight better than lying alone and being always so afraid. Wondering what it was about me that caught his eye, I pushed away any thoughts that I was simply to him a convenience, and indulged instead the notion that I could be seen as actually pretty, that there were far worse going the road than me and men could still look and feel like smiling at what they saw. And on those wakeful nights when doubt started to fester, I decided that it might also have been my accent that had piqued Michael Egan's interest. Set against the impatient bark of the city accent, my voice possessed a definite sweetness, and was something else again in a tune, gentle and wistful. Back on Clear Island, my mother had often told me that my voice was a leftover from long ago, when the world was still a beautiful place. *Álainn agus cineálta* – beautiful and good. My looks, such as they were, my still-young age and the music of my accent were what I had to offer, and although I feared the likes of me could be had ten a penny along the city docks of any wet night with a ship in port, I hoped that whatever had turned Michael Egan's head would prove enough to keep him wanting.

Saying *no* to him was terribly difficult. He'd been trying me from the start, from the first time I stepped out with him, and I resisted, as I had to, laughing, acting offended, fighting him off, until one Sunday in September, after we'd gone a few miles out into the countryside and stopped a while to sit on a wall and eat the cheese and onion sandwiches that I'd talked Elizabeth into making for us. Once we were comfortable, he produced a bottle from inside his coat, drank a deep swallow and then offered it to me. I caught the smell of whiskey from an arm's length away, and hesitated, but with three days of only light duty while Mrs McKechnie was in Belfast for her sister's funeral I had room for a little indulgence, and when he urged me on, pushing the bottle against me, I decided there was no great harm in chancing a sip.

I'd tasted whiskey just once before, while washing up after some visitors to Mrs McKechnie's house, draining the dregs of glasses left abandoned by the acquaintances of her husband, and in truth I hadn't much enjoyed it, but this seemed different, being in company. So, wanting him to think me a woman rather than a girl, I took a drink and, when pressed, another. If it was like swallowing flames at first, then it soon spread through me with such pleasing warmth that I was able to give myself over to it and after a while to savour it, knowing that the house had no demands on me this night, and for once demanded no early start. I relaxed and found comfort in how the autumn light began to swell ahead of dusk and took on that burnished glow. When Michael Egan leaned in, put his arm around me and began to nuzzle at my ear and neck, I tried to push him back but showed little enough resistance apart from a cough of nervous, pleading laughter, and then his mouth was against mine, awkwardly for the first few seconds until I caught my breath, his lips cracked, his skin rough as sand against my cheeks and chin. That's what I'd remember, that coarseness, stinging me, scraping me but in a way that was not entirely unpleasant; that and the reek of him. He'd spent from early that morning through into the afternoon out hunting, as he'd told me he did most Sundays, trudging across fields and through patches of woodland with his brother and their hounds, away northwards from the worst of the city's slums in the casual hope of getting a rabbit or two. And hours on, in the same clothes, the same grey wool shirt and navy sweater, he carried with him the sweat of those exertions, the fibres layered with a sour vinegar stench. I wanted to pull back but couldn't because of how he had me gripped, his left arm dug in between my right arm and side and the fingers of his free hand kneading my shoulder, and when he pressed his mouth down into the crook of my neck again I raised my face and, through clenched teeth and with my lips drawn back into a grimace, inhaled little sucks of air. When he released me, finally, it was only to breathe, and his face was flushed red across the cheeks and his eyes were wide, with their focus stuck in some middle distance, and for a moment it crossed my mind to run, though I knew he'd have caught me, thinking it all a part of some game or using the whiskey as an excuse to pretend as much and maybe to wrestle me to the ground. But even while I was contemplating escape he was on me once more, easing me down from the wall but pressing me against it, and when he kissed me I again filled up with the taste of him, the sickly taste of the whiskey that he'd just swallowed the last of and, beneath it, seeping through, the rotten tinge of a festering tooth or abscessed gum. His body shifted against mine firmly enough to hurt, and in order to ease the pressure on my back, because the wall behind me was full of jagged stones, I had no choice but to return his embrace. Taking that for enthusiasm, he began bunching the folds of my skirt into one of his big fists and dragging the hem up over my knee, telling me all the while that he loved me, that I was everything he wanted and there could never be anyone else that he'd feel like this about. Then, to stifle my cries, his mouth went more hungrily at mine, and not knowing what else

83

to do I clung desperately on to what he'd said and was with every free breath repeating, wanting to believe him, wanting it so much to be true.

Afterwards I lay on the ground, my bare legs cold from the grass, feeling as if my stomach had been reefed open. My mind ran slowly, in a waterlogged way, and while I knew on some level what we'd done, or what he'd done, with me and to me, I couldn't yet make an account of it. Through most of the struggle I'd kept my eyes clenched shut, and his relentless and increasingly frenzied whispering pressed so close to my ear that its burrowing itch gave me another reason to want to shake my head and scream. By the finish, partly because the alcohol had gotten the better of me, I'd slipped into some oblivion, and when I stirred again to the world, night had fully drawn. He lay alongside me in the grass, on his back and with his hands laced together behind his head, gazing up at where the stars would have been if a skin of cloud hadn't spread across the sky and talking in slow, almost absent gasps about what a grand girl I was, and how he'd never before met my like, not the entire length and breadth of the city. Then, because he was tired too, he lapsed into silence so that the only sounds were the leaves of the field's rowans and wych elms stirring in the easy night breeze and among their branches the rustle of a restless owl or bat. When he did rouse himself to get up, he stepped just a few paces away to where the grass was longer, and leaned with one straight arm against the wall. His urine came slowly, with hesitance at first but then in a surge that carried all the ferocious hissing of a cornered cat. I listened to the long flow, keeping my eyes closed and feeling overwhelmed. And that, for me, was the night: angry sounds folded into layers of blackness.

'Come on,' he said, at last turning back to me, and from his pocket drew out a rag that had clearly been serving him a long time as a handkerchief. 'Get yourself cleaned up and I'll walk you back. The old woman will think you've gone on the run.'

I took the rag and wiped myself, which made me feel somehow worse, though I couldn't have explained why. Not just the fact that the cloth was dirty, I suppose, but maybe also the casual way it was given. When I went to get up, he stepped forward and took my arm, though I didn't need or particularly want the assistance, and when he realised that he moved back again to where he'd been waiting and looked on while I rearranged my drawers, fixed the skirt of my old dress into place down over my knees and wrapped the wool shawl across my shoulders. I didn't realise that I was still gripping the handkerchief until he reached out his hand for mine, and when I pressed the cloth into his palm he made the kind of sound that I could only imagine accompanied an expression of deepest disgust, and flung it to the ground. I stooped, out of habit, to pick it up, not knowing what I'd done wrong but thinking that I could wash it when I got back to the house and return it to him when we next met, and

I only then became aware of the blood, thick as phlegm and clammy to the touch.

'Just leave it,' he said, his voice tight. My mind pictured his mouth as a stab wound, a slit. Seconds passed, with me still down on one knee on the ground, until he realised my confusion and maybe also my fear, and he cleared his throat and added, in a more gentle tone, that it was all right, that this was what was supposed to happen the first time, the blood, he meant, and that he was sorry but he thought I'd have known. This time I did let him help me up, and he took my arm with a gentleness that would have surprised me if I'd been thinking straight, and asked again, stupidly, if I was all right. I told him that I was, feeling that my voice was not mine at all, and we got out of the field and started back towards the McKechnie house, taking the road as slowly as a pair of lost dogs, neither one of us speaking but he still linking me, carrying me, almost, taking all the weight I cared to give, until half a mile or so out from the house, just where the road straightened out after some ten minutes of tight bends, when I shrugged free and stopped.

He was still close enough that I could have reached out and touched him, but just at this part of the road, with the trees caging us in on either side, their branches creaking above us in the wind, I was able to make out nothing more of him than his looming silhouette.

'I'll go on myself from here,' I said.

He seemed smaller when he spoke again. 'It's all right, love. I can come up as far as the gate with you. We won't be seen.'

'No, it's getting late, and you've a fair walk back. Barrack Hill is it, you said?'

'Thereabouts, yeah. Well, all right. If you're sure, so.'

It was clear that he had something else to say, and I wanted to hear it but was afraid too that it wouldn't be what I hoped or needed, so I attempted after a moment to cut him short by moving past him. But his hands were still quick even if the rest of him was not, and he stepped partially across my path and caught me just above the elbows, his touch considerate while at the same time making his strength known. 'Nancy,' he said, just that, just my name, as if it were somehow enough, and when he leaned in to kiss me I met him on the way and folded my arms up around his neck, needing him to put life back into me, needing him close.

That was our beginning, and over the following months our Sunday encounters became an unmissable weekly routine. With nobody left to me in the world, I soon came to long for these meetings, and to ache for him, for Michael Egan – because that was how I thought of him: never as Michael or Mick, as others called him, but by his full name – and there was not a minute of my day that didn't stir with the image of his face, grinning in that familiar way, the crimp in the left corner of his mouth setting his features off balance and inflecting every moment with a slash of sarcasm, which some felt bordered on the cruel but which I found endearing. And such was my appetite for him, and my desire, that on a couple of occasions I let him lure me into the storage shed set half an acre back from the house, after he'd arrived to cut the grass or to dig out a new flower bed. Acting reluctant, pretending I was afraid that we'd be caught, though I knew the shed door was angled away from the kitchen windows and that no one could see us, I'd allow him to take my hand and drag me inside. The air in that shed was stale with damp peat, canvas sacks of cement and the salty musk of mildew, but he didn't care about any of that and neither, really, did I, especially once he'd gotten his trousers unbuttoned and leaned me across the heavy workbench over which, for my benefit, he'd spread his coat. The pain of the first few seconds had me biting down on the pad of my thumb but it slowly became everything I wanted it to be, and by closing my eyes I could deepen the sense of what was happening, trying to make these moments a part of me forever – the intensity of the feeling, the beating of his body against mine, his panting voice repeating over and over how beautiful I was. Then, just as my own breath was starting to catch, he quickened and pulled suddenly, violently away, leaving me with a gasp of utmost desolation until I felt him against me once more, his thighs against the backs of mine, and after some further heart-beats his voice again, blown out now to a hush, thanking me and telling me how much he loved me and always would. I remember in particular these moments from the first time for us in that shed, feeling never more connected to another soul and never more certain in my life of a God in His heaven, and because my dress was still pulled up around my ribs and my drawers still down around my ankles, the cold lick of an unexpected breeze passing across my exposed parts put such a shiver through me that I can still recall the chill of it, all these years on. And as I lay there with the heavy black wool of his old coat against my skin, thinking myself impossibly happy, I tried not to move so that nothing would change. But soon enough, everything did.

The first sign of something being wrong was waking with the need to vomit. I wasn't concerned, though, because since leaving the island I often came up out of sleep feeling confused and laden with ropes of the past. Smells seemed the slowest to dissipate, and with them their attached anxieties, and I've always suffered from a nervous stomach, with nausea never at a far remove.

By the third or fourth morning, Elizabeth had noticed. She looked at me in silence, then sat me at the kitchen table, half filled a cup from the kettle of water that had just started to warm over the fire and stirred in a couple of teaspoons of honey – an old cure, she said. I sipped, as instructed, and she waited by the fire, her milky eyes fixed to my shadow. A week later, when my condition persisted, she came and put her hand on my shoulder so that I had no choice but to face her questions. 'Who's been at you?' she asked, in a voice that was neither gentle nor cruel but simply curious. 'Is it that gardener? That Egan fella? If 'tis, girleen, then you've a sight of trouble ahead of you.' She read the signs in my face. 'It is him, isn't it? I'd have backed my last ha'penny on it being. I've seen him, bad as my sight is. Coming up to the door, eyes big as apples whenever you're around. Sniffing. Like your ass has jam on it. He's got some neck, that fella. And him already tied, too.'

I forced stillness into my expression. What she was saying made no sense to me. When I could, I told her, without much insistence, that she was mistaken, that I was the last girl in the world to set the men's heads turning, me with such a plain look and not a pinch of fat anywhere on my bones, but she just smiled, showing off the three or four upper front teeth that remained to her, a smile surely far better suited to meanness than to loving, and said that men were known to make do with a fair slice less than what I had going once they got the right answer when they asked their question.

'What do you mean, tied?'

'Why? Didn't he tell you?'

'Married?'

She hesitated. 'Not married, I don't think. Not yet, anyway. But as good as be damned. At this stage, it's only a matter of the shotgun.'

I shrugged, as if this news was nothing to me and I was simply keeping up my end of the conversation.

I continued to drink the honey water in my glass, which I needed every day now, but this morning the remedy didn't seem to be taking. My stomach churned, and I only kept myself from being sick on the scullery floor by concentrating on drawing air in sharply through my gritted teeth.

'I only know,' she said, 'because a cousin of mine lives a few doors away from him. Up the hill from the South Gate Bridge, that side of the city. He's the talk of the place, has been for years, so she says. And I've seen the woman a time or two. His intended, I mean. His fancy piece. She has a few years on you, but she's not bad-looking and does, it's true, have a nice bit of shape about her. And as far as I know there's a child, too, maybe more than one. But if what he's already got at home isn't enough for him, then likely as not he has them spread all across town.'

In hindsight, it seems ridiculous that I could have so widely missed the point of what she was saying and already taking for granted. But my age was my excuse, and the innocence that came from living the majority of my life up until then in such remoteness. After my mother died, two and a half years earlier, there'd been little left at home for me and not many reasons I could think of to stay. Everywhere I looked held some reminder of what I'd lost. Family, friends, hope. Getting away meant grabbing the chance, once the August storms had blown through, to cross in one of the fishing boats to Baltimore, the mainland town closest to Clear Island, carrying my scant possessions – a few saved coins, some dried fish, biscuits, a can of milk, and my good dress, which had come all the way from America as a gift to a neighbour and, finally, when there was no one else left to wear it, was given to me – all bound up tightly in my mother's shawl, sitting in a twisted position at the boat's prow and struggling all the time to resist a backward glance, knowing for certain that I'd never see my home place again. I remember how a stiff breeze churned up the black and silver water, and a fine salt spray came up over me as we cut through the waves, and how the fishermen heaved the oars – old Pa Sullivan and his brother, Tim, who in their young days, it was said, had once lost their bearings in a dense summer fog and rowed clean to the most southerly point of Iceland. They were gone for close to a month and had been given up as lost, but few believed what they had to say on their return, though they brought a haul back with them as evidence, oilskin coats and hats, and a blanket knitted in a herringbone style that nobody on the island, or across on the main-land, had ever seen. The doubters suggested that they'd only made it as far north as Arranmore or maybe, at a push, Tory, and had likely been fooled by the heft of those northern accents into thinking they were listening to a different tongue, but for years after people still gathered around them at the least opportunity to hear their tales of blond giants and beautiful blue-eyed women, of land as green and rich as any valley the length and breadth of Ireland, and of drink so strong and sweet the brothers had made it more than three-quarters of the way home before starting to sober up. The morning of my leave-taking, I could hear from my position at the prow of their boat the strain of them behind me dragging their oars in a grunted rhythm through the waves, and was glad of the spray to cloak the tears that filled my eyes, thinking of how these brothers must have been when at their best, and thinking about all those of the island who'd never had the chance to wither with age.

After a few days spent in and around the docks, gutting and cleaning the morning's unloaded catch for the fish sellers – to keep me sheltered in one of the Baltimore doss houses until I was able to get myself set and straightened out – I learned that some of the surrounding farms had wheat in need of harvesting. With most of that area short-handed and the demand for labour high I was able to take what work was going, and moved from one farm to another, spending long days in the fields, hacking my way through the ripe acres or gathering and tying up sheaves to dry, staying on for as long as they'd let me linger.

I passed a couple of years this way, working an area's farmland and drifting slowly but ever eastwards, to Skibbereen first, then Rosscarbery, then Clonakilty and Bandon, without any plan other than to eventually reach Cork city, and with the seasons my only concept of time's passing. Because I didn't eat much, just some gruel, a heel of bread, a cup of milk and on good days a bowl of soup, and because I never asked for more than space enough to lay down, the farms always found use for me. Most of the time I felt wretched, but what I had in wandering was no more difficult a life than any other I could have imagined, and no worse certainly than I'd previously known, and my youthfulness kept alive in me some semblance of belief that everything would pass, that nothing was forever, and that there had to be something better up ahead, perhaps even something approaching happiness. Now and then it was necessary to fight off or escape some old man who'd catch me unawares and get me cornered, but meeting that kind was rare enough and, in general, the roads, fields and milking sheds were safe ground, especially since the farmers' sons and the young field hands, those who could have inflicted the greatest harm, had already cleared out in search of better, on ships bound for Canada, Boston or New York. The occasional dances that were still put on outside of one town or another tended to be dry, awkward affairs, with fiddled and whistled music that suited no one's mood, and with the girls to one side of the floor and on the other side the men, stooped, grey-faced types mostly, staring across the trampled saw-dusted ground as if assessing cattle, every one of them middle-aged and widowed.

That was the world as I'd come to know it: an existence of barley fields, potato drills and cold, lonesome nights in dour hovels lining narrow streets. And yet when I closed my eyes it was Clear Island I continued to see, still undimmed two years on from leaving, the undulations of the land and the sea's immensity a reminder of my own life's scant significance. It took from afternoon until late the following morning to walk in to the city from Bandon, following the road in the direction of the sun's rising, carrying a billycan of water and some cheese and cold biscuits wrapped in a piece of cloth, stopping an hour at a time every few hours to rest and, come nightfall, settling down in a quiet roadside spot just outside of Ballinhassig for whatever sleep would come, until dawn put me on my way again. But nothing I'd seen of villages and towns could have prepared me for the squall of a city's crowd, the confusion of criss-crossing streets, the reek of the river, the open sewers gullying the roadsides and, in the mouths of countless laneways, the rats that watched me with small shining eyes and moved only when I made myself a stamping threat.

I spent my first few days identifying the big houses and going from door to door in search of work, surviving on handouts and what I could salvage from kitchen waste, before withdrawing again, once the hour grew late, to the city's outskirts, where the land opened up into fields, woodland and riverbanks. Though the notion of being surrounded with life was what had drawn me eastwards, once here I yearned for solitude because the city at night terrified me, the gaslit streets made long with shadows, and the women outside the dockside taverns selling themselves to the sailors for small change. The most miserable among them were truly wretched, in their forties but looking half as old again; others were no age at all, four-teen, fifteen, maybe, but still coarsened by the time they'd been living this way. I kept to a safe distance in hurrying past, but often still heard from one bridge or another the singing west Cork sound of their voices raised in drunken laughter, the tone so suddenly familiar I could almost have placed the very village they'd come from, and the thought of recognising some of the faces made me nervous of paying them too much attention.

Then one day, Mrs McKechnie found me scrubbing a vat of bedsheets in the yard of a friend of hers, after I'd turned up at the scullery door and caught a week's work for a cot in the pantry and a bowl of dinner at night. In the brusque fashion to which I'd soon become accus-tomed, the old woman gave me the job of keeping her home, making no mention of wages, not actually offering the position so much as instructing me on her sundry demands and expectations. The girl she'd been employing had recently taken off for England, she explained, most inconsiderately leaving her in a bind, and so I was to be given a fortnight's trial, after which she'd consider making the situation permanent.

When my bleeding still hadn't come a month on from the start of the nausea, there was no longer any doubt. I'd missed a couple of my Sunday meetings with Michael Egan but had seen him on the previous Tuesday, his scheduled gardening day, though I was careful to stay indoors and only stole glances from whatever window

I happened to be near. He didn't seem at all upset that I wasn't available for him, and went about his work in the usual fashion, without hurry, methodically figuring out what needed doing and in what order and then setting about the task, comfortable in his skills. I made sure to be out of the scullery when he arrived at the back door a little after noon, and from the hallway, straining to listen, I could hear him talking to Elizabeth in an easy tone that people rarely used with her, and laughing in the slow, endearing way I'd come to know. I waited to return until ten or fifteen minutes after he'd gone, and made nothing of it when Elizabeth mentioned that he had called, the now-familiar smirk chiselling deep, ugly dimple holes into her lardy cheeks. I shrugged and, acting distracted by the burden of my workload, hurried back out of the scullery and up the stairs, where I spent as much time as possible cleaning out and setting the fire in Mrs McKechnie's bedroom, work that I'd have had to do anyway, though I usually left it wait until after dinner had been served, when things began to quieten. But all the rest of the day I was conscious of the hours ticking by, and finally, no longer able to resist, I slipped outside to the garden just before he was due to finish and let him steer me behind some shrubbery to steal a kiss, explaining as best I could while his mouth went at me and his mucky hands grabbed at my skirt's hem that I'd felt under the weather the previous Sunday but would be there, in our usual place, the coming weekend, if he was still of a mind to see me.

'Well?' Elizabeth asked, as soon as I came back inside, so I knew she'd been keeping a check on us from the window. As poor as her eyesight was, she'd caught him taking me by the arm and urging me into cover, and had easily enough imagined the kiss.

'Well, what?'

'What had he to say for himself?'

I looked at her with as blank an expression as I could forge.

'So, you didn't tell him. Well, I can't say I'm surprised. You're not the first to be fooled by thoughts of love, and you likely won't be the last. But don't worry. He'll know soon enough. We all will, and there'll be no more need for denials.' She looked triumphant and yet at the same time full of pity for me, and was somehow easy with such a contradiction. 'Did you ask him about the other woman, at all?' she added, as an afterthought that had delayed itself only for effect. 'Or are you hoping he'll tell you of his own accord? Because my advice, sweetheart, is not to save your breath on that.'

There are periods of my life that I find it hard to speak of, because they've left me with a shame that, if openly acknowledged, will taint my family for generations to come. And there is neither comfort nor redemption in knowing that there were plenty like me making the same mistakes, or that others played a part in my fall, because however innocent I might have been, I can't plead a defence of ignorance. I was foolish, yes, and guilty of being too trusting and too easily led, but the truth is that I was also excited by Michael Egan's animal masculinity, and by the way he always made me feel just that little bit afraid. There can be no excusing how he identified my vulnerabilities and took fullest advantage, but I was also responsible for what happened, being weak as I was, giving way to such compulsions when I knew them to be wrong, letting myself be persuaded.

Once my condition was known, I had no chance of being kept on. Mrs McKechnie ran a clean and proper house, and I'd put her in an impossible situation. She wept in telling me to go, though with anger rather than compassion, and Elizabeth, looking every day of her age, leaned against the windowsill, with her head hung and her fat arms folded high and tight across her chest, despising herself for giving me away, and sorry for it. No quarter was given. My week's pay waited on the scullery table, what I was owed but not a farthing more; and too numb to cry, unprepared as I was for all of this though I'd anticipated such a response, I stood there, hands at my sides, gripping the rag I'd just been using to polish with, and stared at the floor that I'd only an hour earlier finished mopping and which still carried the wet sheen of my efforts, and when Mrs McKechnie at last turned away I cleared my throat, mumbled a thanks that she may have heard but just as likely didn't, and gathered up the coins.

As much as I've buried, certain moments from that time have retained a sharpness that can still now slice me open, and take the breath from my chest. Like the way Michael Egan's face had drained of all colour when he saw me on the street, after I'd lain in wait for him in the centre of town knowing he'd have to pass that way home, and how he'd stopped ahead of me, and all the time, until my voice began to lift its pitch, his eyes never once met mine but trawled the street for faces he might recognise among the passers-by. Then, afraid that we were attracting attention, he stepped into one of the side lanes, extending a hand so that I might follow, and supporting himself against the wall of an old archway told me he was sorry for what had happened but that I'd made a bad mistake in not taking more care to mark my times. Because was I that stupid, that I didn't know what the bleeds were? I should have caught it earlier, when something could still have been done, as anyone with an ounce of sense would, because there were things to take, tonics and the like, cure-alls, that could have easily solved the problem. I told him I'd been thinking we could marry, hating how much like a child I felt, and he'd never regret it because I'd do everything I could to make him happy, I'd be good to him, better than any wife would ever be, but he just stared at me, without expression, and then his hand went into his pocket for whatever little money he had, again just a few coins, a couple of shillings and some pennies wrapped in an old, earth-stained handkerchief. It wasn't much, he said, but the best he could do for now. My reaction was to stagger backwards, and I might have dropped onto the cobbles had I not found myself pressed against the other side of the archway. My hands flailed for the wall as I fought to keep back tears, and the ground between us, though we were still within touching distance of one another, seemed suddenly gaping. But he continued to keep his hand open before me and finally, because of how that made me feel, how small and whorish, and just wanting it to stop, I reached out and accepted what he had to give.

'Don't come after me again, Nancy,' he said, and waited until I looked up at him. 'I mean it. You don't want to try me.'

Just then, it would have taken nothing for him to step in, without giving me time to call out, and simply smash my head open against the wall, and I often wondered, later on, whether such a thought had crossed his mind. But he didn't need to turn violent; what he said was enough. He continued to stare at me until he was certain his meaning was clear, then turned and walked off, out of the lane and away with the passing crowd. And watching after him, I couldn't have known that more than a year would pass before I'd set eyes on him again, or hear word from him, and that by then he'd have slipped far from my reach, after marrying the woman who'd already borne his first child, also a girl, though whether or not he did so with the barrel of a shotgun to his back, as Mrs McKechnie's old cook had suggested, I can't say and don't imagine I'll ever know.

*

In the weeks that followed he dominated my thoughts, and the grind of my sad situation failed to keep the fantastic at bay because in my mind I could still escape, and still imagine myself living a good life. After Mrs McKechnie put me out, my modest savings kept me just a few weeks, and with a baby on the way I had no choice but to seek the shelter of the workhouse. Naive as I was, I'd assumed my stay there would be brief, that I'd soon be found again by Michael Egan and set free. But once it became obvious that I'd been thoroughly abandoned to my fate I tried to keep him from my mind, accepting that nothing good could come from it, and because I couldn't cope with how little our kind of love mattered.

Mamie was born in late March of '72, a frail infant, especially after my milk, of which there'd never been quite enough, had dried up. But she was placid, having quickly learned that tears were a wasted spill. It took me the better part of a year to regain our freedom, that long until I was able to prove to the authorities that I had the wherewithal, that I'd hoarded enough of the pennies I'd earned scrubbing in the laundries. And once we were out of the workhouse, and I'd found us a place to live, a cramped tenement near the North Cathedral in Blackpool where we shared a floor with four other families, survival became yet again all that mattered. I did what had to be done in order to provide for her, shameful things that I could not regret, as much as I hated myself for them, because I knew they were neces- sary. I'd slip out of the house once Mamie was asleep and make for those places where I knew men with money in their pockets would be, keeping my eyes low so as not to glimpse faces, and trying not to think as I was pressed back against a wall or, if they preferred, faced into it, tasting the red-brick dust in my throat while the rest of me was being taken charge of, my skirt pulled up and hands and fingers roughly feeling the way.

If Mamie stirred when I returned home in the hour or so ahead of dawn, I'd sit on the floor just beneath our room's window, rocking her gently in my arms, and when she cried I'd put my mouth beside her ear and sing the old island songs that went back to the time of her grandmother's grandmother, humming the words I'd forgotten, keeping on until Mamie drifted back to sleep or until the room brightened to the strains of morning light and, with them, the small attacking racket of the birds. With those songs calling home to mind, I'd sometimes imagine how it would be to take her back down west with me, setting off for the islands because there at least we had a home to call ours, with walls enough to block the wind, and if I was to be a bitch for rabid dogs anyway then couldn't I be that on ground that was at least known to me? But while I indulged in the thought I knew it was something that could never be, because having to live that way at home would have brought shame beyond bearing, and here, at least, I was a stranger.

'I wouldn't have believed it,' Michael Egan said, sobering up fast. 'Not of you. Never of you.'

He'd been in one of the pubs in Blackpool, along Peacock Lane, and had come outside with two of his friends, them dragging him loosely by the coat sleeve but he being easily enough led. Two women that I knew to see, and to pass a few civil words with, were idling beneath the gaslight nearest the pub's door, and when the three men came close they moved eagerly alongside, each taking a flank, and within seconds had peeled away his companions, grabbing an elbow, as they'd learned to do, and leaning in with little giggled kisses. After a few words of negotiation the newly matched pairs slipped off into the night, one of the men singing in a slurred but melodic tenor as he went, the leftovers of whatever song had been going in the pub, and a moment later one of the girls barked with the shocked laughter of having been suddenly and intimately grabbed, as the drunken were known to do. I was leaning with my back against a high brick wall further along, far enough out of the glow of the gas lamp that I could be seen as a shape but not easily identified. I could see him, though. Michael Egan. At first he seemed lost, but then he took some money from his pocket, brought the coins close to his face and counted, and I knew he'd seen me, or seen someone, a woman, and was deciding whether to go back inside for more porter or to spend what he had on this kind of comfort.

I felt myself turning cold, and then numb, and I almost ran. Some of it was shame but as much was anxiety, over what he'd say, what he'd do. In the months since getting out of the workhouse, I'd had it all: men who punched me just to have my face bleeding when they kissed me, wanting that wet heat and the sense of my pain; men who liked to get their hands around my throat and to squeeze so tight that what started out for them as a game quickly had me kicking at them and, often for days after, with trouble swallowing; and even one – a priest, young, gentle-voiced and fatly handsome, well known among the girls of the area – who tried to get me to act the boy for him. Those men who knew their business and went about it quietly and without fuss made in a terrible sort of way for an easy night, which was what I always hoped for, but they still had something deeply amiss, not particularly because of their fleshly wants – which, given all I'd seen and had done to me, I believed to be very much just part of the natural male inclination, the beast in them letting loose – but because of how they wanted to believe that what we were at was a gentle and loving act, closing their eyes and picturing the faces of others that they kept trapped in their hearts but could never have. Afterwards, in pressing the money into my hand, sometimes – if they had it, and if they needed some show of gratitude from me – with an extra farthing or ha'penny, I'd see in their sad-eyed smiles that they were just as damaged as the ones more violent or depraved, and recognise that I was still nothing to them, not a woman with life in my body, and feelings. Seen by day, living with or beside them, they must have seemed like everyone else, and at home they were most likely decent men, kind, honest, good providers. Yet outside of these few snatched minutes in late-night alleyways, their true natures remained concealed.

Michael Egan came forwards into the shadow but refrained from touching me, and silence lay between us until he cleared his throat. Given all I'd been called in the past year and a half, first in the workhouse and then out on the streets, it took more than words to cause me pain. But not from him. From him a punch in the mouth would have been easier.

'What about the baby?' he said.

'What do you mean?' I couldn't see his face, yet could picture him, his expression plain from the hard tone of his voice.

'I mean, what was it? A boy or a girl?'

'A girl,' I answered, feeling a quiver within the words. 'Mary. After my mother. Mamie, I call her. She's a sweet thing.'

'So we did something right, then. I'm glad.'

I shook my head. He couldn't see the gesture but I felt sure he'd sense the movement, and the meaning. 'We didn't. She's what she is despite us. Despite you.'

For a second, his breath seemed stuck. 'Yeah,' he said. 'I'm sorry about that.'

'You're not. You're not capable of being sorry.' My calm, despite its bedrock despair, surprised me. 'It didn't have to be the way it was. You could have helped. You could have at least kept me out of the workhouse. Christ.

Prison can't be worse. It's no place to bring a child into the world.'

'Don't be putting all that on me, now. You played your part. Or did I make the baby by myself?'

'The odd shilling would have kept us going. You think I want to be out here, pulling up my skirt for men like you?'

'As I recall, you opened your legs for me with little enough persuading.'

Suddenly then, he stepped closer, angry but also seemingly hurt, as if he had some right to be. I felt the press of him against me and almost cried out when his hands clenched my arms at the wrists and spread them wide apart so that my body, remembering, yielded to him. I turned my face away towards the gaslight, but couldn't stop the onslaught of his details: his breath heavy with its porter reek, skin a mixture of sweat and something of more subtle spice, and the intensity of his glare, the way he'd always looked when watching me, how his eyes shone and the bones of his lower face shifted in jerks beneath his rough, unshaven skin. I despised how he continued to make me feel.

'Where is she now? The baby?'

'I left her sleeping. The other women will listen out if she wakes.'

'That's decent enough of them.'

'They do it for her, not for me. There's no other way.'

I might have said more, such as how there wasn't a single night in returning to the house after putting in my

107

shift either down here or outside the pubs up around Shandon that I didn't feel as if demons had made a nest in me.

But I was too afraid for further words.

I was expecting an attack, I suppose, a lashing out, rather than the kiss that came instead. His lips pressed to my cheek, and the feel of it made me want to cry out, and beat and kick at him for the suffering he'd caused me, but still my body answered of its own accord, straining against him only for more. I hated him, yet famished as I was for kindness, or affection, or even just a fleeting moment of tenderness, I still craved his touch. And that frightened me more than anything else. Ahead of us, another pair of men came out of the pub and moved, hands in pockets, into the cast of the gaslight. The girls who'd gone with Michael Egan's friends never took long about their business, practised as they were, and these two, knowing this, seemed content about waiting. While I watched them, glad of the excuse to be able to turn my face away, Michael Egan started kissing me again, my neck and cheek, working towards my mouth, and then one hand was grabbing at my skirt, and when I felt the fingers and palm of his right hand crawling up the inside of my thigh I froze. I wish I could have fought, but something in his touch bothered an old weakness in me, and then, just as happened when he first had me up against a wall, I felt my legs edging the merest inch or two apart. But when he said something, sighing the words against me, I failed to respond, and seemingly because of this he drew his hand away and stepped back, so harshly that I felt sure he was about to run, or to start punching. Instead, he went into his pockets, and drew out what money he had. Given what I'd become it seemed ridiculous to hesitate, and yet I did, just long enough for him to clear his throat again and to tell me that I should take it, that it wasn't much but he hoped it would help. The coins were warm from his pocket, and when he folded my hand into a fist around them I just about had time to wonder exactly what it was that he thought he was buying, before he turned and walked off back towards the city and was lost from sight.

I remained where I was for several minutes, unable to move, still clenching the coins in my hand. One of the men beneath the gaslight stared across at me and nudged his companion, who asked, in a voice full of laughter, if I was on my own. When I made no answer they seemed uncertain about what to do, and I realised that despite the middle-aged way they were dressed and trying to behave, they were actually no older than me. But before one or the other of them could stoke up courage enough to approach, the other girls came up out of the nearby lane and, seeing easy custom, began the kind of vulgar, shrill-voiced talk that soon had the young men laughing again. I wanted to be sick. I dropped down onto one knee and my stomach contracted, but because I hadn't eaten all that came up was a rope of bile. The effort of the dry heaving brought tears to my eyes, making the world around me a swimming mess and stripping me of all sense of direction except for the ground on which I was kneeling.

I'd done all I could to forget Michael Egan. I'd prayed for him to be taken from my mind, initially to Christ and the Blessed Virgin, and then, in desperation, to those older gods I remembered occupying the talk of the old people back on Clear Island whenever storms threatened, or the shoals were slow in coming. But there was no forgetting that, as crowded as the city was, we could never have had more than a mile separating us at any given moment. The likelihood of us falling across one another's path again had surely been strong, though I'd refused to believe it would ever happen.

Once my nausea passed, and supporting myself as best I could against walls and railings, I made it back to the house, lay down beside Mamie without troubling to undress, and closed my eyes. Instantly, he filled my head again, and it was as if our time apart had counted for nothing. The angry pain of old wounds after a while gave way to other memories, of the two of us laughing together in Mrs McKechnie's garden, quietly so as not to be overheard, and of letting him take my hand, pleasuring in the strength of his grip, when he walked me back along that tree-lined road on those Sundays with night-time closing in. Other, greater intimacies, too, like how strong and assured he was with me in the shed or in the fields, and the look in his eyes, a wild, dog-like shine, when I cried out at the shocks he sent through me, and as much as I wanted to wish him dead I still felt lit up by the thrill of having him back in my life, certain that, married or not, he wasn't done with me after all, that we had more ahead of us and that there'd be other days, other nights, maybe other walls to lean against, now that he knew where to find me.

When I was a child, my mother often told me that we'd been a hundred generations on Clear Island, one branch or another of us, and on the day the last one of us left, the island would sink out of grief to the bottom of the sea. And at sixteen, as I sat in the prow of the Sullivan brothers' boat, wanting more than anything to risk a backward glance, those words kept me afraid. For the entire crossing, my mother's voice sang loud inside me and so truthful-sounding that, had I turned my head, I felt sure I'd see the cliffs crumbling in on themselves and their blankets of gorse and heather flushing the stony-grey water with shades of purple and pink and gold. And worse still, that there'd be scatterings of my dead watching after me from the strand, thin-shouldered and forlorn, knowing I'd never return, that this was the end. On Clear I knew the faces in every doorway and the family names that occupied every plot of graveyard earth, I knew the slopes and climbs of the fields, where the best berries grew and where the ground birds nested, and I never slept a single night without the sighing of the running waves.

By the time I was born the worst of the starvation had passed, though few enough would have known it.

The blight had been at its most widespread two or three years earlier, when those who still had strength enough, or who'd already lost what for them had been most worth losing, got themselves away, and too many among the ones who stayed ended up gasping their last in fields or roadside dikes, or on the sandy shorelines that they'd already stripped of kelp and carrion.

It's only dying. That's what my mother used to say. This was the late sixties, and I was in my teens and she was reaching towards her own end. But while we were a sight better off than we'd been, a lot remained unchanged. For most of my childhood we fed on scraps. Everyone did, everyone I knew. Potatoes again, since the tubers had stopped rotting to black pus in their pits, and fish when we could get it, herring or mackerel, depending on the time of year, when one or another of the men came back following a day and a night on the water with catch enough to be able to share a bite. My mother made soup from the heads and bones, and from seaweed, too, whatever we could rake from the shallows, and I'd spend a couple of hours every morning down among the rocks collecting mussels, crabs and periwinkles, in defiance of the priest – a stern, long-faced man from Baltimore whose green, half-hooded eyes kept looking for something out over the shoulders of the people he was speaking to – who'd tried drumming into us that the flesh of any shellfish was detestable, and to eat of it an abomination against God. He was heard but mostly ignored, because he wasn't one of us and wasn't of our world. And if we were offending God so much, my mother said, under her breath, angrily, then He should have put more our way than just suffering. We continued to live as best we could, doing what was necessary to keep on, but years of that took its toll on her, and by the time I reached ten years old, she was needing to lie down several times a day. Sometimes the pains in her head grew so severe that I thought my own mind would snap from having to listen to her cries and small pleadings, and all that kept me from running away to the far end of the island was the certainty that if she found herself alone she'd have done something drastic to free herself from her agony. So instead of bolting, I squatted at her side and squeezed her hand for as long as the attacks took, three, four hours on the worst days, trying all the while not to look at her face with its bunched, discoloured flesh and the froth gathered in the corners of her mouth, and whenever a fresh stab of pain dug in she braced herself so that her body arched upwards from the waist. 'It's only dying, love,' she'd tell me, once the attacks had subsided, and though she couldn't open her eyes she'd turn her smile, sad and lovely, towards the sound of my voice. That she was still just in her mid-thirties seemed impossible because for me she was as permanent as the ancient standing stones around which I used to play, but as I've since come to realise, time is not the right measure of a life. 'We're passing through, that's all. And the end comes easier and more quickly for some than others. This is just a step along the way.' I'd miss her when she was gone, she often said, but I'd go on, because that's what living was. And she hoped that when my time came I'd have somebody who'd miss me too, because that was as much of a mark as any of us could hope to make.

The end, when it did come, was like the sun going down. No howls or tears, nothing but a gentle, inevitable drifting away. After half a week spent asleep, the air for her simply stopped flowing. I was beside her, weary myself from having sat up all that time and faint from not having properly eaten in days, and I couldn't have said how long she was gone before I noticed, though the flesh of her face was already cold when I leaned in to kiss her. Her eyes had fallen open, which meant that during her last minutes she'd woken. In the candlelight, she looked better than she had in a long time, maybe better than I'd ever known her, the muscles of her face having relaxed into more comfortable lines. I combed back the tangles of her hair with my fingers, and lifted her head just a little so that her mouth didn't hang open, and it was only after I'd remembered to lean in and say an Act of Contrition for her that I began to cry.

I got her buried with the help of some neighbours, and though there was a priest present he had sense enough to keep back, understanding that he had no real business here, neither he nor his god, and he let us say our own prayers. It took a while to get over, the idea of being so entirely alone, and people around me tried to help but there was only so much anyone could do. I resisted as long as I could, then finally gathered my few belongings and left the island. As frightened as I was to go, if I'd remained I would surely have met the same slow death that my mother had suffered, but with nobody to comfort me and to see me into the ground, unless I gave myself up as wife to some old man, and in the hope of bearing children yielded to a life of mismatched appetites and needs only ever half met. I wanted better than that, and going seemed like the one chance I had of finding something more. Unlikely as it was that I'd ever return, Clear Island still filled me up every time I closed my eyes, its strands and boreens and the faces of all who'd gone before, and if I was less for having had them stripped from my life, then I also knew that I was nothing without the memory of them.

There were any number of roads and street corners that I might have chosen to work, and plenty walls that I'd already leaned against in the months I'd been whoring, but a week on from the shock of having encountered Michael Egan again I returned to Peacock Lane. The pubs were plentiful around there and the lanes offered such convenient shelter, but it was only on seeing him coming up the road, hands sunk into his coat pockets, that I understood I was laying myself out where I knew he'd be first inclined to look, were he ever of such a mind. That night was a cold one, threatening rain, but I had just a loose grey wool cardigan on over a shirt missing half its buttons and an old linen vest. I'd been out only half an hour, securing my spot ahead of closing time, but had my arms tight across my chest and was already shivering.

I caught sight of him making his way up Clarence Street from the city, bent into the breeze but taking his time, lingering at the mouth of each lane he passed and peering into its black pit, and it was not until he was twenty yards from my corner that he noticed me.

'You're here again,' he said.

My heart began to race. I looked up at him. 'What do you want?'

'I don't have much.'

He opened his hand to show the few coins. My throat hurt from the pulse that was driving through me. I looked around at the otherwise empty street then stepped backwards into the lane. He hesitated before following, and when he tried to take me in his arms I stopped him, felt for his hand and the coins, and only then let him embrace me. This time when his mouth went for mine I didn't turn my face away, and I closed my eyes and for those few seconds had two years of my life back, and just a little of my innocence, and I was once more – until I thought better of it – in love. That was a word I'd learned not to mention, but longed again to feel. He seemed to have convinced himself that what he was doing was noble, that he was sparing me from myself and other men, and neither could I help but try to make something more of what was happening than in my heart I knew it to be: a trade, a service rendered for the few meagre pennies I

116

was worth, and no different than any other deal I bartered with the drunks who stumbled from the closing pubs or with the sick types who'd temporarily escaped their lairs. It was a pretence, but one easily and eagerly enough played by both of us.

After we'd done, I let him walk me back to the house, neither of us caring that it was taking him out of his way. He didn't try to touch me or reach for my hand, and the whole time, through ten, fifteen minutes of walking, we spoke very little, but for the first time since my fall I didn't completely hate the soul inside me.

'Don't be thinking the money's meant as payment,' he said, at one point, and I looked away because it was easier to accept his words than to have to read into them. 'It's a bit of support, that's all. To help out with the baby. I know it's not much, but if I can manage it every week maybe it'll be enough to keep you out of the lanes. Because you won't last long at that, Nancy. It's no kind of life.'

'No,' I agreed, as if we were discussing something I'd started into by choice. 'Not much of a one, anyway.'

And that's how it went. Mamie and I made do with what money he put our way, and he grudgingly agreed to meet in the same place, just there on the corner of Peacock Lane, at the same time every Saturday night, so that if he failed for whatever reason to turn up I could still get enough business done to ensure our survival. While some of his seeking me out was, I chose to believe, kindness on his part, though a compassion likely fuelled by guilt, it was still work of a sort for me, because he never failed to get his ten minutes' worth in the lane, having me lift my dress in bunches around my belly while he pressed me against the wall, sometimes keeping so leisurely a pace that I thought we'd never reach our end, but on other nights going at me with such frenzy that he'd have no sooner started than he was done, in gasps of humiliation that were hard to tell apart from sobs, and afterwards couldn't bring himself to look me in the eye. However it played out, though, I convinced myself that with him it was different than with the others, he being the only man I'd ever kept any kind of feelings for, so my heart, despite how I might have wished it otherwise, was more involved.

For the first three or four weeks, until late into November, we stuck to our routine, and while initially I shrugged away his promises and tried to prevent him from getting too close, my disgrace being still raw and kept so from having to live daily with its consequences, a few weeks of his persistence was all it took for him to wear me down and turn me to his ways again, I wanting so badly to believe him, and to believe in him. I'd heard him speak his words before, of course, but a born fool only ever learns the most cruel lessons, and when he suggested that we meet on a different night, and earlier, because of how tough a time he was having trying to justify being out so late, I only hesitated for show before agreeing. The money he slipped me was never a lot,

118

certainly less than I'd have earned on a regular week, but I was able to cover our share of the house's rent and keep us just about fed, and to be escaping the life I'd come to know, not having to hate the sight of myself in a piece of glass or wince at the mention of my name, was worth a little extra deprivation. I wanted to believe I could move on from what I was, that people's memories would grow faint and a time would come, maybe in another town or city or on the other side of this one, when I was no longer defined by the things I'd had to do. Soon enough, Michael Egan and I were getting together twice or three times a week – sometimes just for a few minutes and only to chat and maybe kiss a little, sometimes spending entire afternoons together, the three of us, he taking Mamie in his arms, I linking his elbow, for a walk northwards out into the countryside, the way we used to back when we'd first met, out past the last of the houses and away from the city, and the risk of his being seen and maybe reported. We were of course very much in the wrong, he being a married man and a father to his own legitimate children as well as to Mamie, but I couldn't have stopped if I'd wanted to, and neither I'm certain could he. Not while he had a choice. It meant so much to hear him admit he'd made a mistake in not doing right by me and was deeply regretful for it, and my thoughts were full of him getting me into a field, as he always wanted to, or some disused forge shed, telling me the entire while that all of this was just like it used to be for us and the time which had fallen between, all the bad things I'd been through, could be forgotten now; talking this way as he dropped his trousers below his knees, sighing as if breath could only be taken and spent in words, pleading with me to talk about how much I needed him, until he was ready to get me down in the grass and part my legs for him to lie between. He made a show of giving me his money as soon as we met, so that it didn't have to feel like payment for what he knew he was soon to have from me, and I took the change, meagre as it was, and thanked him with gratitude. After being alone for so long, the past would fall away and the future stopped mattering, and there was only the day around us and these moments spent together.

The support he was giving me, scant as it was, caused some strain in his life, and forced him to work a few extra hours in the week in order to make it up. Still, we went on without trouble because I put no demands on him apart from the few coins, and he was getting what he wanted, which, to be crude about it, was considerably more than his money's worth. But by February, four months after he'd come back into my life, I realised I was pregnant again, and already several weeks gone. I wasn't always regular, especially during the cold parts of the year – one of the consequences, I'd heard some of the girls saying, of malnourishment – and there'd been times, back when I was still untouched, that extra weeks would pass without a hint of bleeding, so at first the signals were easily enough ignored. The vomiting let me know for certain, the same early-morning nausea I'd suffered on Mamie, but I persisted in my silence through into March, clinging to the increasingly foolish hope that the problem would still simply rectify itself, or that all of this was just a delusion, a false alarm.

Towards the end of that month, as I lay back in a field with him beside me and with Mamie asleep at my other side, swaddled in a shawl, I raised enough courage to ask, in a tone as casual as I could make it, what he thought would happen to us if another baby were to come along. He didn't answer, and at first, because there was no change in the rhythm of his breathing, I wondered if he might have drifted off to sleep, as sometimes happened to him after we'd done with one another. But he wasn't asleep. A minute or two later, I felt him sit up, with that sudden, disturbing tightness of a bad decision being made, and when I opened my eyes and shielded them against the glare of the chalky sky I saw him staring down at me, hands in fists at his sides. Earlier, as he was trying to wrestle me out of my clothes, he'd passed a remark about my stomach, laughing but with serious – and, I'd felt, somewhat unfriendly – eyes, about how well fed I was looking since he'd come back to me, and whether it was time for him to consider easing up a little bit on the amount of money I was getting. For my own good, he added, pulling me to him, and because he already had all the fat he needed at home and didn't fancy me going the same way.

'Why would you say something like that?' he asked, without need of an answer. He was exposed from the waist down, his skin pale as pig fat and his thing still lazily heavy. And then, angrily, and with fear, too: 'Oh, Christ, Nancy. Oh, you stupid bitch. How could you let that happen?'

'How could *I*?' I said, lifting myself up onto my elbows. Tears started to build, and my voice went shrill the way it always did when I was terrified, and loud enough that it startled Mamie awake and into tears. 'You think this is down to me? You think I made myself pregnant? Is that what you think?'

Michael Egan glared at me but said nothing. I could see his cheeks filling up and emptying and knew his pulse must have been racing and his blood aflame. Then, abruptly, he gathered his trousers and stepped into them, the left leg first and then the right. While buttoning his shirt he half turned to consider the miles of fields, watery shades of green and grey divided up by ditches and old dead-looking trees. I reached for Mamie, shaken by how fragile everything about the day had become, and remained where I was, my cardigan pulled across my chest but still otherwise naked and nervous to move.

'How far along are you?' he asked, with his shoulder still turned from me.

I shrugged, not caring that he didn't see. 'I'm not sure,' I lied. 'Two months, maybe three.'

'So something can still be done.'

'What do you mean?'

He glanced across at me. 'There's stuff you can take.'

'You mean kill it?'

122

'Kill what? No. That's not what I'm saying.'

'What else can you call it?'

'It's solving a problem, that's all. Come on, Nancy. What do you think is going to happen? That I'll leave my wife and children for you and your bastards?'

I hadn't thought of consequences, hadn't let myself, because every time I tried I started to come apart.

'Well, I'll tell you something right now,' he said. 'We're done, you and me. This business.' I could hear his harried breathing, which made me think of a saw-blade tearing in and out of lumber. Then the air caught in him, and I braced myself. 'Anyway,' he added, after a short but terrible silence, 'how can I know it's mine?'

'What?' I sat up. 'How could you say that? You know damn well it is. You know I've not been with anyone else since we started up again.'

'And I'm supposed to just believe you, am I? How could I have been so stupid? For all I know, you've been knocking your nights out the whole time. But I suppose this is all for the best. I mean, I'll be lucky if you haven't got me red rotten with the pox.'

Now I did weep. For a few seconds my lungs refused the air. He just looked on, still with gritted teeth but smiling now, bitterly. I waited for that grin to drop, for him to recognise the monstrosity of it, and when he didn't and I could no longer bear the sight of it I turned away, found my clothes and quickly dressed, then once more gathered up Mamie, who'd stopped crying and taken to watching. Her face nuzzled into the crook of my neck and I felt the small loving heat of her against my skin, and in that moment was overwhelmed with a dread that gave my tears a more frightening reason for their spilling. Without glancing back at Michael Egan I started with our child down through the field to where the crumbling wall gave out onto the narrow road. Town was an hour's walk away, and I wasn't sure, given what had happened, that I had the strength to carry Mamie so far, but I was determined I'd make it. I set off, and though my head was full of noise I focused as best I could on the road beneath my feet, and on the baby in my arms, and how the weight of her soon began to strain the muscles of my shoulders and back, a burden that had become once again entirely mine to bear. For the first mile or so, as my fear continued to grow and the reality of my situation became clear, I kept hoping to hear him behind me, hurrying to catch up and wanting to apologise and make amends. Sometimes the road would bend and either the wind in the budding elm branches or something small scrabbling in the ditch would make the kind of hurried sounds that I could almost convince myself were footsteps, and once or twice I stopped, needing a minute's rest, and actually turned my head to look, ready at the right word to forgive. But the road back that way was always empty, and finally, with the sound of the breeze in the trees accompanying me most of the journey back to Blackpool, I stopped expecting him.

*

The money I'd managed to put by didn't last, and within weeks we were once again destitute. For as long as I could, I deluded myself with the idea that he'd think better of all that had happened and come back to me, that my revelation had simply shocked him into saying the things he'd come out with, a natural enough reaction if not a noble one, and he surely just needed some time and a bit of space to get his mind right. But in my heart I knew.

Going back on the street was not an option. Built as I was, I'd already begun to show, though so far to a degree noticeable only in my naked state, which nobody got to see, and I reckoned I had a good month yet, maybe longer, before people could have told at a glance. But showing or not didn't alter the facts of my condition, and I was repulsed by the thought of offering myself up again to a slew of strange men, and of inflicting that on my unborn child. I lay beside Mamie in our cramped corner of the Blackpool tenement, all too aware that the nights left to us under this particular roof were numbered and fast slipping by, and fantasised about crossing the city to Barrack Hill and going from door to door in order to locate Michael Egan, recounting my predicament to any who knew him, any who'd listen, just so his wife would see the kind of man she'd married. But such a thought was fleeting, and left me feeling empty. Because after two years of living together, no wife needed to be told who her husband was; she'd have known only too well the bad as well as the good of him. And even if she did listen to what I had to say, nothing would change. They were just like everyone else, with their own mouths to feed and rent to pay, and it was no concern of theirs whether I took myself off either to the river or back to the workhouse. Michael Egan had made his mistakes and walked away from them, twice now with me and who knew how many times with others. That he could do so without repercussion was the way of the world.

From the moment Michael Egan cut us off the workhouse awaited us again, but because I knew that surrendering to it would bring about as harrowing a time as any I'd endured, I avoided it until there was nothing left, not a penny, not a drop of milk or a crust of bread to keep us going. In the house, the other women found reasons to occupy themselves, and those who did look my way quickly lowered their eyes. They pitied me, but they also knew what I was, and they clung that much more tightly to their husbands and older sons, and steeled themselves further against me, deciding that I was entirely the cause of my own downfall.

On that final free afternoon I sat for hours gazing from our first-floor window, not expecting anything to happen that might yet save us but still, I suppose, hoping. Then, when I could wait no longer, I gathered Mamie up into my arms and readied us for the slow walk across the city and out along the Douglas Road, not wanting to arrive at those gates without some glimmer of light left in the sky. And from there I stepped into an emptiness as lonesome as any unmarked grave and, for a long, long time, died.

In Douglas, three years from that day, I was a stranger, and could live as such. I chose this village because with its mills and abundant farms and big houses, there was honest work to be had. And if I was a curiosity for being husbandless then the few fictions I chanced to tell, such as how he'd been a soldier killed in Africa, was good enough for most. Though I'd by then been up in Cork six years, the fact that I'd spent more than half that time locked away in the workhouse had kept me more or less invisible. And I had my accent, and could fall back into short flurries of Irish, half in panic, half as cover, which tended to shield me from more intense scrutiny and gave me an excuse for my missing pieces, and my strangeness, in every sense of that word. It helped that there were others living locally, men and women of my own age and older, who also hailed from down west – Clonakilty, Dunmanway, Skibbereen, Bantry, Beara – and who'd blown into Douglas seeking work in one of the mills and to escape from how bad things had been back at home, and I suppose they saw in me enough of themselves to be friendly towards me when they could, or to at least not be wicked. And if a few of the older women in the village, those who'd seen a bit of life, sensed a tendency, the whorish part of me, then they also recognised during those first weeks that I was a woman now devoted only and entirely to the children in my care. At the workhouse they had taken Mamie away from me, as was their custom with children who were past toddling age, and that period of separation was an agony from which I would only ever half recover. By the time we arrived in Douglas, united again and finally free, she was nearly five and my younger one, a boy I had named Jer, was two and a half. Frail as feathers because of how little food we'd been given in the workhouse, he was a serious and mostly silent type, oddly thoughtful, as if cursed with a wisdom beyond his years, but afflicted too with the kind of explosive temper shocking to see in one of such a raw age. A soldier boy, some of the neighbouring women along the terrace often said, smiling and shaking their heads as they watched him grow and telling me there'd be trouble yet with him and that I'd have a war of my own to fight if I hoped to keep him out of a uniform.

That first year passed in a blur. The Douglas we found was a village divided into two distinct sides, East and West, with the Protestant and Catholic churches, and their graveyards, taking up most of the land in between. The West village was shaped by two rows of terraced homes filling the half-mile's worth of space between a pair of mills, situated next to a fast-flowing river known locally as the Pond Bank; while the East village, which carried the tramlines from the city, had more broadness about it and opened out onto a wide estuary after a mile's stretch of marshland. Only three or four miles from the city, the place felt snugly self-contained. Those who didn't work in one of the mills found ready employment as maids or farm labourers with the big houses, and so ends were easier met there than in more wildly rural areas. We found lodging on the city side of the West village, in a small house on Bog View that was giving shelter to a family named the Colemans. Our space was the loft, and the Colemans were friendly enough people who welcomed any small contribution towards the rent. I paid our way through scrubbing work in a few of the houses along the Passage Road, and during the summer months picking potatoes and turnips for the local farmers. And we got by, though the workhouse had taken quite a toll on my body and mind. Having to be on my feet for hours at a time would cause my joints to swell, and when walking home I'd often have to stop and lean a while against a wall. The pain was real but frustration played a part, too, by now understanding my lot and realising how unlikely anything about it was to change.

There were still men who showed some interest in me, though not for any kind of honourable reason, especially considering the baggage I carried. Even if they believed me a widow and therefore still decent, having heard the story I'd been spinning, the fact that I was so lacking in prospects quickly sent the attentions of most elsewhere. And the ones who remained were to be avoided. Types too wide with their smiling, too wanting in the moment to help, to be friends, and who laughed when pushed back, deciding to make a joke of my refusals so that they felt free to try again at other times and in more forceful ways. I'd come across men like this in the workhouse and, if the truth were to be told, among those in charge of us, a few women too, people who could only properly smile when they had someone else weeping, and it was worse in there because quiet corners were always to be found, and the consequences of refusing an order or a demand – a day without food, a beating, or some other unspeakable cruelty – tended to trickle down to the children. Like the others, I did what I had to do, blocking it out in the moment and burying it to a depth that defied easy recollection. But that was then, and what went on in that place remained behind its walls. Out here, on Douglas's back roads or in the farmers' outhouses, I could refuse in roars and, despite my size and relative frailty, I had some fight in me. And thankfully, because such men so feared being overheard but also because they adjudged me not worth the trouble, I was left largely alone.

Then one evening I returned home, weary from a few hours spent picking potatoes, and Mrs Coleman came in from the scullery wiping her wet hands in a piece of cloth, and indicated a letter waiting for me on the mantelpiece above the unlit fire. Without opening it, and though I'd never seen more than a few words written in his hand, I knew instantly who it was from. My insides shifted, and for a few seconds everything dimmed around me so that I had to feel my way to the stairs beside me to sit. The older woman didn't speak until I looked up at her and shrugged. Then, with some hesitance, and having cast a glance back towards the scullery to see for certain that her girls were still busy with their chores, she took the letter from my hand, slipped a thumb behind the seal and drew out the note.

Dear Nancy, it read, as if mere weeks had passed instead of the four years that it actually was since we'd last spoken. *I hope you and the children are well. I always had such a great fondness for you, and I think of you often. The time we spent together was some of the best of my life, and I treasure the memories. Maybe you do, too. I know some mean things were said between us in parting, and I regretted not being able to remain friends, but maybe time can smooth any grudges you might feel. I am writing to you now because I would like to see the children. Mamie must be five or six, and I am interested also in meeting the other, a boy, I believe.*

Just that, and without an attempt at a proper or conciliatory ending, a simple signature, *Michael Egan*, full and cruelly formal. I took the letter when she handed it back to me and stared at the marks that I knew represented words on the page, and it was only when they started to run that I realised I was crying, and I was relieved then that Jer and Mamie were outside on the terrace, caught up in some chasing game with a few of the neighbouring children, and that the men of the house, Mr Coleman and the two older boys, were still at the mill. Mrs Coleman lingered before me a minute longer, not

131

sure what to say now that her suspicions had been confirmed, then slipped back into the scullery to take up her washing duties, helped by her two eldest daughters, neither of them that much younger than me but who by comparison seemed like girls still. And if they'd heard any of my commotion or had some sense of what was going on, I could only be grateful for how they pretended not to notice.

I sat on the stairs for a long time, then wiped my eyes with my fingertips, feeling angry at myself for even thinking about what the letter was asking. I'd outgrown the hold he'd had on me, having suffered too much to willingly open myself up for any more of that nonsense, any more of him. But a part of me did still want Michael Egan to want me, to know that I was worth something, that I was a real person, made up of better than just the flesh he'd once so hungered to grab. While the life I'd had to bear had toughened me it had also made me weak, fragile as a wren's egg, to the point where I felt hurt to the quick by every murmured remark or the way I thought I was being looked at.

I stared at the letter until I could no longer bear the sight of it, then tore it into strips and added it to the unlit fire. After a sleepless night spent turning the whole business over in my mind I decided I'd given enough of myself to Michael Egan. His words remained with me but I was able to keep them mostly at bay, which might have been why, some three weeks later, a second letter caught me by surprise. This time, again read by

Mrs Coleman, who'd become out of necessity the one person I could trust though we weren't in fact all that close, it didn't waste words. *Nancy, You will know from my last letter that I want to see the children. Bring them to the corner of Barrack Hill and Maypole Lane on Sunday at two o'clock. I'll pay for the tram fare. If you decide not to come, I won't write again. This is a chance to have them meet me. Don't spoil it for them.* And, once more, signed in full: *Michael Egan.*

This time, I didn't hesitate before tearing it asunder, and I wasted no tears on it, choked as I was with anger at the idea of him offering the tram fare, after he'd let me walk, infant in arms and with another on the way, across the full breadth of the city to the workhouse. Here was a man who'd talked about tonics I should take, poisons, to cure me of our problem, and who, after having his way with me in that field, had cast me aside as the whore he'd turned me into, the wreck. Mamie and Jer could have starved or frozen to death for what little damn he'd ever given. And even now he referred to them only as *the children*, still not willing to recognise them in any kind of open way as his.

By the Sunday morning, walking with my usual reluctance up the Churchyard Lane to Mass, letting Mamie stroll along beside me but keeping a fast grip of Jer's wrist, he being the type of child who, given the least opportunity at escape, would either take it or fall down trying, I'd grown steadfast in my refusal to give in to this second letter's demands. But in the church, at that tranquil early hour, as I sat on the back pew and closed my eyes, something about the sound of the other parishioners' shoe heels on the aisle's porcelain tiles caused me to temper and to reconsider my position. In spite of my grudges against Michael Egan I began to worry about what he had insinuated in his letter, that I'd be doing the children a significant wrong by keeping them from him. It scarcely mattered much to them at this age, but a few years from now, years that would pass quickly, they'd have questions, and would feel a need to know at least something of who they were. Most of the truth would always have to remain out of bounds, but I decided that they deserved to grow up with the memory of meeting him, if only once. Before the priest had made it from the sacristy to the altar, I'd gathered and herded them back outside, Jer happy, regardless of why, to be free again of the church's shadowy chill, but Mamie old enough to feel confused, and maybe a little bit afraid. Before I had a chance to talk myself out of it we hurried back down the Churchyard Lane, crossed to the East village, caught the next scheduled tram, and arrived in the city a few hours earlier than necessary.

When we did finally meet again, he and I barely spoke. Until it was time, I'd walked the children around the streets, stopping at windows of shops that were shut for the day but still displayed their wares, suits and dresses, pots, kettles, cups and plates, shoes of shapes and colours I'd never have imagined. And at half past one we followed

Main Street past Beamish & Crawford brewery, the air smouldering in a sweet reek of yeast and slow-brewing hops, and crossed the South Gate Bridge, stopping a minute or two at the low wall to watch the Lee, black as porter slops, frothing as it carried the weir. And just as we started up the incline to Barrack Hill I saw him, waiting some fifty yards ahead, where the road branches off towards Maypole Lane, his back propped against the corner, and his arms folded across his chest, as easy with himself as ever. All morning, once the decision was made, I'd been thinking about how I'd feel on being confronted with him again after so long. Angry, I'd have said, if pressed. But at that first glimpse what I experienced most strongly was a terrible sense of emptiness, and a conviction that, measured against the sight of him, I was nothing. Suddenly it was hard to breathe. If I'd been able I'd have turned and run, but instead I kept leaning us into the hill. Then, noticing us, he lifted himself forwards from the wall and moved into the centre of the footpath, big hands hanging uselessly.

'Nancy,' he said, without much to his tone. 'You came. I wasn't sure you would.'

I wanted to answer but found that I had nothing to say, and almost in the same instant the chance was gone because he dropped his eyes from mine, crouched down and began speaking to Mamie, asking if that's who she was and telling her that he hadn't seen her in quite a while but she really hadn't changed much, and he'd still have known her anywhere.

135

Ignored entirely, Jer clung tightly to my leg until I put my hand on his back between his little shoulders and ushered him forwards a step or two so that Michael Egan was forced to notice him.

'And who have we here?'

I felt myself hesitate. 'This is Jeremiah. Jer. He'll be four next month.'

'Jeremiah?' Michael Egan looked up at me, his eyes narrowed and not because of the light in the sky. I met the stare without flinching, and after a moment it was he who looked away. 'Well,' he said, 'let's go if we're going. I'd say we'll get a drop of rain before the hour's out.' He straightened up, and I was again struck by his size, which I shouldn't have forgotten but somehow had. Though slender enough still across the chest and shoulders, he had filled out over the years, and above us he was somehow – as emphasised by the awed way the children were gazing up at him – towering. Then he turned and set off, and I had to walk quickly to keep pace, and the small ones, on either side of me, had to hurry into a skipping run. He led the way in long steady strides, a hundred yards or so up Maypole Lane, then took a right turn, followed by a quick left and another right into a maze of slum houses and tenements and a road called Blue Coat Lane.

'A mate of mine lives here,' he said, after herding us through one of the heavy doors and into a narrow hallway that smelled of damp. 'In future, whenever we're to meet, this is where you'll come. So when you're leaving, pay attention to the way. But if you do have trouble finding it next time, ask anyone around here for Mulgrave. There's nobody else by that name in these parts. He lets me use the place when I need somewhere private.'

He opened another door then, giving onto a narrow front room, and reached for Mamie's hand. As if in response to a question that had not quite been asked, she released her grip on me. 'You can wait here or in the back room,' he told me, and I nodded, not sure why I was so anxious, but remained where I was, unable to move, after he'd eased the door shut just inches from my face. When Jer began to pull at the hem of my skirt, I lifted him in my arms, feeling his fear, and together we listened to the murmuring from the other side of the door, shapeless yet with a calm and gentle tone. But after a few minutes, at a burst of my daughter's laughter, as if she were being tickled, I could no longer restrain myself. With three quick warning raps with my knuckles on the wood, but without waiting for a response, I pushed my way into the room. He was down on his haunches, elbows on knees and the fingertips of one hand touching the floorboards for balance, with Mamie standing directly before him, caught in a smile and gripping a small paper bag of boiled sweets. 'I thought you might like to speak a few words to this one, too,' I said, still with Jer in my arms, his scabbed knees straddling my right hip and one hand curled around my neck. Michael Egan stared at me, then shrugged, as if giving me permission to put the child down.

'So, you're Jer, are you?' he said, taking on a tone that was almost mocking, though I didn't feel that its intent was deliberately cruel. 'That was my father's name, too. Imagine that. Well, it's a good strong name, and if you turn out half the man he was then you'll not have done badly.' Transfixed by this attention, Jer's mouth hung slightly open, a string of dribble spooling from his chin, and when this strange man smiled he hesitated before smiling back.

'I'm glad you came, Nancy,' Michael Egan said, after we'd gone out again into the hallway and were setting to leave. He'd taken his coat off and had left it in the front room, draped over the back of a small wooden chair, which I took to mean that he was set on staying a while. He handed me a few farthings to cover the cost of the tram, then from his trousers pocket drew out his handkerchief and unwrapped it to reveal four shillings and some pennies. 'Go on,' he said. 'I've been putting it by. Take it. Hopefully it'll help out a bit.'

In no position to be proud, I took the money, though I couldn't bring myself to thank him for it.

'I must say,' he added, after clearing his throat, 'you're looking well.'

'I'm not,' I said, keeping my hands busy with the children. 'How could I be, after where you put me? And after what you put me through?'

'Ah, the workhouse is it that you're talking about?' he said, and I could hear the smile in his words without having to look into his face. 'Sure, there's plenty pass in

138

and out of that place and survive it. Didn't they keep you fed and watered, and didn't they give you a bed to lie in? Which is a sight more than many have. And wasn't it better than you being on the streets of a night, opening yourself to every drunk with an itch? You'd be red rotten by now if you'd kept that up.'

If he was trying to goad me then he'd succeeded.

'But wasn't it because of you,' I said, trying, for the sake of Mamie and Jer, both of whom were staring, to keep a civil tone, 'that I was on those corners in the first place? Any kind of a decent man would look out for the children he'd fathered. You can cod all you want about the workhouse, but you don't know what you're talking about. Not the first thing. You never put yourself out a hair for anyone. Others might not say it but I will. You're a filthy hateful bastard and nothing else.'

'You've that wrong, Nancy. I'm not the bastard in this house.'

His smile widened at that, and his voice was easy, as if to indicate that I was supposed to take his words as a joke, and I think if I'd had a knife in my hand I wouldn't have hesitated in running it through him, even with the small ones looking on. I'd have plunged it into his stomach, and when he dropped I'd have set to work on his eyes. But there was no knife, and my hands hung empty at my sides, squeezed into fists, my bitten nails pressing crescents into the skin of my palms, and all I could do was draw deep breaths until the blackness that had come over me drew back, and once I was steady again I turned, unlocked the door and, pushing Mamie and Jer ahead of me, stepped back outside into the cold of the afternoon and the rain that had just begun to fall. When he called after us with a *so-long*, Mamie strained to turn but I refused to stop, and when she raised her hand in a small, nervous wave I knew it was in answer to whatever he was sending her way.

On the journey back to Douglas, watching the rain, which was now coming down heavy, streaking the tram window's glass, I tried to make myself believe that, despite everything, it was good we'd gone, because the money, little as it was, would help. The things he'd said, and his smiling face as he'd spoken, hurt me, but not as much as it would have a few years earlier, and if that was mostly because of what I'd been through, then it was also partly because I felt hardly anything for him now. My great dread had been that I'd start to fall for him again, that he'd laugh the right way or say the right thing and have me coming helplessly apart before him. That would have been the end to everything. There'd have been no surviving further disgrace, and I knew that if I stumbled then the children were lost, too. So seeing him again, sharing the hallway of that house, the two of us barely a step apart from an embrace, and feeling no more desire than I would for any stranger, came as an immense relief. Until then I hadn't realised how captive I'd been, not to him as he actually was but to the thought of him, the ideal that I'd conjured and been unable for so long to let go of. But no more. I got to see up close how he'd changed, taken on age, greyed and turned pallid, and yes, he was tall still but clearly sapped of some essential ferocity, as if something bad was working inside him, something with teeth. If the money was some attempt to buy a way back to me, the first hack at digging a path once more into my life, then I'd become weathered to such approaches. I'd learned to accept living lonesome, having seen that the world was full of so much worse. And I had my family, my children. Our situation meant we'd struggle and likely never have much, but I was determined that we'd be enough for one another, at least until they were grown and ready to fly the nest. And in that way, we'd survive.

Years slipped by. I continued to take what work I could pick up until settling into something more permanent – regular hours and steady pay in Lane's hemp mill, separating the harvest ahead of the winding process. A few years later, I crossed over the road to take up a position for an extra thruppence a week as a darner in O'Brien's woollen mill, alongside the Tramore River on the city-side of the village. And so we lived. Almost without my noticing, the children put inches on their bones and pounds on their flesh, and grew up steady and strong. Mamie, from the youngest possible age, played mother while I was out and whenever they happened to be off from school, and Jer, so given to bouts of outrage, happily fought her battles as well as his own. They shouldn't by all rights have fitted together as easily as they did, but they seemed to live for one another, as if it was just them against the world. And once I had steady money coming in, we found a better place to rent, moving down from the loft at Bog View and taking a room in one of the houses backing onto the Pond Bank; and then, encouraged by the security of the woollen mill's work, finally reaching for a place of our own, a two-room cottage named Forge View over in East Douglas. The house was out towards the Finger Post, perched on the roadside directly opposite the small but busy blacksmith's premises that it was named for, and to our backs the millworkers' sports and social club, St Columba's Hall, and the open half-acre of the Hall Field. A shell of a place, barely walls and a roof, but manageable for the amount of rent I had to pay and something we'd never had before: a place to consider ours, a real home. I had always woken with the dawn, to the cries of birds, but for the first time in years, maybe in my entire life, dread was no longer waiting. Taking just a couple of minutes, I could lie still, beneath the coat I'd spread over me as a blanket, open my eyes and listen for the linnets and warblers stirring into song in the trees and hedging along the roadside, and to the sighing of my loved ones asleep beside me. And I could smile.

Throughout those years, and although we only occasionally saw him, Michael Egan remained a presence in our lives, especially for Mamie, with whom he forged a seemingly genuine bond. Their encounters remained sporadic and awkwardly brief, lasting for no longer than a few minutes at a time in the front room of that house on Blue Coat Lane, until Mamie entered her teens. When letters arrived beckoning another meeting, I always went along, and for the first few years waited either in the hallway behind the shut door or, if the weather was fine, outside on the road. Later, once I'd grown reasonably comfortable with the arrangement and the children were of an age where they could be trusted, I cut them loose at the bottom of Barrack Hill and let them make their own way the last few hundred yards without me, Mamie squeezing Jer's hand less for his security than for her own. I'd watch after them until they'd slipped out of sight, then cross back over the bridge to idle at shop windows along Main Street to pass the time until their return.

By the time I was forty, by any measure of my heart I felt thoroughly old. But a casual glance would have noticed little difference, apart from the few pounds of fat I'd put on and which I knew suited me, rounding my shoulders and thickening my limbs, giving me a comfort I had never previously possessed. As someone who'd borne hunger the entirety of my life, I had at last enough to satisfy me, potatoes, bread and butter, porridge, milk, the occasional piece of meat or fish, and once in a while an egg. During those early visits, when Michael Egan showed the slightest bit more than a passing interest, I put him in his place. I knew he was testing the ground between us for embers of old fires but I think

143

there was also some need on his part to prove himself still the man he'd once been. Far from appearing disappointed at the rejection, though, he simply shrugged, as if to suggest that a fellow couldn't be blamed for trying, meaning it as a compliment, and let it go at that, I think with a certain amount of relief because he was by then displaying firm signs of his own age, which stripped away quite a bit of the swagger that in his better days had so defined him.

Knowing him as I did, his advances were expected if not desired, and he wasn't alone in trying his luck. In the mill, too, men still glanced my way when they came into the darning shed, either pushing carts of wool or collecting the fines, the more brazen of them chancing a remark in the hope of some little encouragement, but I was cold as pond water to any words of that sort and after a while they stopped trying. A few of the older women scolded me for that, telling me that I could ease up a bit and nobody would think the worse of me for it. At my age, they said, there was still plenty of life to be lived, and while it was true enough that most men were little better than mongrel pups, neither were they entirely without their uses, especially once winter set in and the nights turned cold. I was decent-looking, these women assured me, women I came to think of as friends, the first since childhood that I'd really known. A fair enough sight and still with plenty of good years ahead of me, and if I was of a mind to look around, they said, they'd happily steer me right because there was no one living within two or three miles of the village in any direction that they didn't know. I thanked them when they talked like this, but told them, in a voice so low it was almost swallowed up by the racket of the loom, that I was finished and done with men and romance and that my days of looking around for them were long behind me. They considered me then in sadness, knowing I was serious, and from that point on such talk was dropped and never again raised.

I accepted being single, but there was nothing heroic or brave about that. It was simply that my own wants were no longer a priority. The children always had to be fed first, and kept closest to the fire on cold nights. And when enough time passed and they no longer needed me quite as they once had, the part of my heart that could have benefited from the other kind of love had already dried up. My mind swarmed with memories of long ago, not all of them bad despite how things had gone. But the good recollections among them were fragile, and by middle age all that properly remained to me were my children, though neither one of them was a child any longer.

Mamie married Ned Spillane in '03. Against my wishes, it must be said – though she was already thirty years old by then, a factor that prevented me from interfering. And in time she bore babies of her own, two boys and a girl, each beautiful and healthy. I am there to help as much as I can, and she and I often spend hours of the day sitting and talking, or busying ourselves alongside one another with washing or some such chore. I need her as she once needed me, and being with her eases at least some of the guilt still hanging over me from years ago, when the authorities had separated us in the workhouse my second time in, farming her out with a five-pounds-a-year incentive to any family willing to take her on. I'd done my best to wean Jer, and wept away every one of my nights until I could have her back, until we could all get out and away and make our life together as a proper family. When that day came, being able to see her again after so long, I was afraid to touch her at first, thinking that she wouldn't know me. But I was wrong. She charged at a run into my arms, calling me mama, and I gathered her up tightly enough that she might have feared injury. I never asked her about who'd taken her, not in all the years after, nor what they'd been like, because enough was said by the glassy way her gaze would sometimes fall; and she never talked about that time – years lost to us that couldn't be regained – except to mention on a few occasions the prayers she used to say for me, asking God to let me come and find her again, words that made me want to burn certain people and places to the ground. She went into Spillane's arms, I think, feeling her own smallness, a woman but still in her heart a child, and that hurts me too, because I see so much of myself in how she used to be, as if I'd set a path that she was cursed to follow.

Jer too knew pain, and more than his fair share, because of some of the places he took himself to. At eighteen he became the soldier that had been predicted for him since infancy, and, handsome in his uniform, he set off chasing adventure, leaving me to endure the fearful days and nights as I clung to his promises of safe return, promises that he somehow, and against all odds, managed to keep. As decent a type as ever walked in shoe leather – a thing said of him by plenty besides his mother – he somehow found time in between all his soldiering to court and marry, a lovely girl from the Passage Road, Mary Carty, and I myself fell quickly in love with her for the way she loved my boy. And this has been another chapter, watching as they set about filling the house at Forge View, Mata first, and now Annie, who is the image of my mother. Looking at her causes a tuck in my heart because of the notion – in an odd way, the certainty – that nobody dies, not really, not when their same blood runs through ever younger bones. She has my mother's eyes: the exact polished pewter shade of the ocean on a winter's day that I haven't seen in the better part of fifty years.

For somebody who'd started out with nothing, and who has walked the roads I have, my old age is closing in more gently than I ever imagined it could. And yet some ends, even when they are natural and to be expected, still feel sudden when reached, and are capable of knocking your soul askew. I am thinking now of last year, a late morning in October, when a tapping arrived at our door. I was on my knees in front of a fire that had been allowed to burn down since breakfast, stirring the ash with the intent of laying in some fresh turf and a few scraps of kindling. Mary sat across from me on a stool, cutting carrots into a blackened pot for the night's stew. Mata was just a few months old, and because he was keeping Mary up most nights I'd been trying to help keep her duties light. But before I could move she got up to answer the door, still clutching the knife in one hand. I remained on my knees and strained to listen but the new voice pitched itself so low that it fell short of me, and after the opening enquiry, Mary's voice fell to match it. Then she stepped backwards from the doorway ahead of a young woman who looked to be in her mid-twenties. A tall slip of a thing, handsome rather than beautiful, most would have said, but still striking in her way, with loose, shoulder-length barley-blonde hair that she tucked behind her ears over and over using the same hand, her left, raking that side into place first and then attending to the other side, turning her head a little to meet the second tuck, an unusual and oddly endearing gesture so quickly undone by repetition that it couldn't but suggest itself as a nervous quirk. I smiled in greeting and she tried to smile back, then seemed to think that a betrayal of some sort and let her expression tighten into a frown.

'Are you Nancy Martin?' she asked, and her nervousness felt amplified by the room's otherwise silence.

I said I was, and sat back onto my heels.

She had on a long beige trench coat that she wore wide open, despite the day being so late in the year, a week short of winter, and the way it hung from her slender body only emphasised her height.

'I'm Liz,' she said, her eyes steady on mine. 'Liz Egan.'

All at once, I knew her. With her broad forehead and a mouth made full by prominent, some would say horsey front teeth, she wasn't exactly the spit of Michael Egan, and the restless way she moved her hands, stretching and straightening out her long fingers as if to chase away some stiffness, had none of his infuriating ease, but now that I knew who she was I could see no one other than him gazing back at me, with that intense way she had of staring. When Mary offered her a chair – the best we could manage, not yet having fire enough to heat milk for cocoa – she nodded and muttered a vague thank-you but remained where she was.

'It's Michael, is it, that you've come about?'

Speaking of him felt peculiar, because I hadn't uttered his name aloud in years. And I couldn't remember ever having used his first name without his last in tow. I didn't want to be on my knees when I heard whatever she had to say, knowing it would not be good, so I put my hand on the wall and lifted myself up from the floor. She made the smallest movement forwards, as if to lend assistance, but checked her step and instead took in her surroundings.

She glanced at Mary, reluctant I suppose to speak of intimate business in front of someone not directly involved, but after a few seconds seemed to accept that it was all right, that it no longer mattered now, and after clearing her throat told us that he'd died during the night, that he'd been sick for quite a while, a year or more, but had taken a turn for the worse only in the last ten days. They could have got him shifted to hospital, and with some proper treatment it's possible he'd have lasted a bit longer, weeks, maybe a few months, but he wouldn't countenance talk of that and said he'd rather die at home, in his own bed. 'Stubborn to the end,' she added, after a heavy breath, trying again to smile.

I understood his reluctance, and despised him for it. The thought of that place, in connection with him, resurrected suddenly and unexpectedly all the horror I'd left buried. The District Hospital straddled the bones of what had been until just a decade earlier the Union workhouse, the place he'd twice condemned me to; and I could think of no more fitting place for him to lie and suffer and finally breathe his last. Ghosts surely walk those hallways still, and the nights must echo with the low beating of so many forgotten cries. Time passes and people forget, either by choice or otherwise, but I'm not sure that places ever can. I'd long since stopped hating Michael Egan, or thought I had, and to discover such feelings still festering and to know that after all these decades I continued to yearn for some kind of balance, a hope that he might experience at least something of what I'd gone through, filled me with shame.

The girl, the woman, Liz, kept talking, her voice cold and full of sighs at having to recount the circumstances of his death for the half-dozenth time that morning, telling us about how he'd been coughing like a rook for quite a while and how, a few weeks earlier, after she'd caught him rinsing blood from his handkerchief at the pump on Cove Lane, out in front of the forge there, he had implored her silence. She'd given in to him without wanting to, realising his lungs were shot and that the point where anything might have been done to save him was likely long past. And because she loved him. Surely nobody wants to betray the people they love, even when doing so might be for the best. She didn't notice that I'd fallen to weeping because she didn't look at me, and when I raised my head, wiping my eyes with the ashen pinch of a thumb and forefinger, I saw that her gaze was stuck blankly to the wall, her focus lagging a second or two behind the actual moment, in that manner only grief can cause.

'My dad,' she said, as if that needed saying, and then Mary was beside her, steering her gently towards the chair. Tears left marks in dropping down onto her coat's lapels. 'I know what he was like, of course,' she said when she could, and she met my eyes and this time didn't look away. 'With the women, I mean. I don't need to be told. He was no saint, but never claimed to be. I'm here because of my mother. She felt you had a right to know. The others, my brothers and sisters, wanted no part of it, so it was left to me.'

There was so much to say, and so little that we could bring ourselves to speak of. Mary pieced the basic facts together without the need of explanation, and when the infant, Mata, began to cry in the bedroom, she got up and went to attend him, leaving us in uncomfortable silence.

The girl, Liz, turned her head towards the bedroom door, which had fallen shut. 'Boy or girl?' she asked.

'A boy,' I said. 'Mata.'

'How old?'

'Four months. And already a handful.'

'Mary's your daughter, is that right?' the hesitation ahead of her words impossible to ignore. So she knew something of us. We had been discussed.

'My daughter-in-law. She's married to my Jer. But I have a daughter named Mary, too. Mamie, we call her.'

'She's nice. This Mary, I mean. She seems nice.'

'She is. Jer's a lucky man to have her. They're lucky to have one another.'

'Did my dad know? About the baby, I mean.'

She continued to study me without flinching.

I shrugged, and hoped anger didn't show across my face. 'I couldn't tell you, love, what he knew or didn't know. I haven't set eyes on him in a long time.'

'Is this your first grandchild?'

'No. Mamie has a boy, and another child due any day now. And Mary and Jer have another on the way, too.' Now it was my turn to pause. Her expression was calm but hard to read. 'I stopped sending word many years back,' I said. 'I suppose because I'd grown tired of not being heard. The fact is, I never wanted much, at least not once I knew how things were going to be. I do feel for your mother, though. Honestly, I do. And for you and your family. I'm sorry for your trouble.'

Each of the girl's slow exhalations made the sound of paper being torn. 'My mother told me about you,' she said.

I nodded. 'I often wondered if she knew.'

'One night, late. The others were out somewhere, at the pub or some dance. I'm the youngest. I don't know if you know this, but there's five of us altogether. But growing up, I always thought something was off. I just sensed it. My father wasn't an easy man to manage.'

'I can believe that.'

'Women would knock on our door. Not often, but too often for my mother's liking. And sometimes in the night I'd hear arguments, her voice high and doing most of the talking. My father wouldn't give much back but he had a strength about him when he did speak. Of a weekend we'd see little of him because he'd be off to one or another of the pubs. My mother, left at home, would sometimes take a drop of gin, and I suppose on one of those nights I just happened to catch her in a talking mood. She told me that there'd been one other woman, in particular, you, going back to before they'd married but still well after they had started stepping out together. She either hadn't your name then or just chose not to share it with me but she did know that you were a fair bit younger than her and had come in from the country to work as a maid in one of the big houses on the northside. And she knew it had gone on for quite a

153

while and that he'd gotten you in trouble at least once, once that he'd admitted to.'

I hesitated to respond. I could have explained what had happened, but that was a part of my life I wanted nobody to know about, because of how it shamed and lessened me. To open myself up in such a way as that, when I'd resisted doing so for decades, would have helped neither one of us. Yet, though this girl already knew more than she should or wanted to, I sensed that I'd regret not giving her at least something of my heart, some few truthful words to take away with her.

'I remember a time,' I said at last, and could feel my voice turning wet again, 'when Michael Egan was the very turning of my world. That was another life, and all I feel now, in this one, is sadness, knowing that somebody who once mattered so much to me is gone. But the truth is, I lost him and had him dead and buried long ago. I'm sad to hear this news, and I'll cry more over it, both for your father and for myself, when I am on my own and have had the chance to let it all sink in. But I also can't feel about it the way I once would have.'

The cottage felt suddenly very small around us. She remained in her chair, and although we were strangers, a couple of steps apart from one another, there was something of an embrace about the moment that needed no further words. I could see from the way she watched me, her cheeks gleaming beneath her wide eyes, that she felt it, too. The connection – whether we wanted it or not.

And then, with the quietest possible reluctance, conscious of intruding, Mary came back in from the bedroom. Having overheard everything, and having recognised the things that had gone unsaid, she looked sombre, not sure quite how to feel or what she was expected to say. Mata nestled against her shoulder, quiet now and content, having had the breast, and Liz, our visitor, dabbed at her eyes again and got up to meet them. 'What a handsome man,' she said, leaning in for a better look, and Mata, caught by the sound of the strange but gentle voice, turned his head and, after a slow heartbeat of hesitation, smiled.

When she put out her hands to him he didn't hesitate. 'Hello, Mata,' she cooed, and tickled him under the chin. 'That's a nice name, isn't it? I don't think I've ever heard it before.'

'It's a pet name.' Mary glanced again, just for a second, at me. 'He was christened Michael. Jer wanted it. He's a handful and a half, this one. Nancy says he'll likely skip the walking altogether and go right to running. Just like his father.'

Liz's leaving kept awkwardness to a minimum. She touched Mary's shoulder, turned to me and pinched her lips in a silent and somewhat relieved goodbye, then went. That was all. She'd been with us barely half an hour but it had felt so much longer, and the questions she hadn't needed to ask were all as good as answered, just as she in her way and with her own silences and stares had answered mine. And in mentioning how deeply

I'd already buried Michael Egan, after having so long ago given him up for dead, I'd saved her the trouble of finding words for the request uppermost in her mind, which was that we stay away from the funeral and leave them all, his real family, to grieve in peace.

As soon as we were on our own again, Mary began to speak, but I barely heard. I was looking at my fingers and noticing that the ash I'd been handling had powdered my skin pale, but instead of brushing them off or wiping them on the skirt of my pinafore, I laced them together and dropped once more, in some kind of finish, to my knees.

III

Nellie

(1982)

When I was young days felt so long, and time seemed so slow in passing. I used to listen to my father talk of all the places he'd been, and dream that I'd travel the world myself, that I'd someday get to walk the streets of London and New York, swim in half a dozen oceans, write poems and sing beautiful songs, that I'd always have in my purse a few shillings more than I could spend, and would be swept away in gales of love by someone tall, handsome and strong in all the ways I desired. I did get to savour love, and even if I had to make do with paddling in streams instead of seas and never travelled further down the road than Killarney, I still got to see and experience plenty of the world – more than my fill, some might say. It might not have been the life I'd have wished for as a girl, but we hold on to what happiness we find. And now, with my end in sight and the clock shedding its hours and days faster than I can count, I've come to understand that there's peace in acceptance.

Happiness for me now is in belonging. I live just a stone's throw from the house in which I was born, with my daughter Gina and her husband Liam, a quiet type, one of those who seem born to work hard, and who keeps the home fires burning with long night shifts in one of the factories in Ringaskiddy. And I have my grandsons to occupy my time – Bill, who's seven now, and Martin, our newest arrival, named for my father's mother's people. My other children aren't far, and we remain close-knit; and I have my village, a place of so many pasts, all interwoven, and where, soon enough now, they'll lay me down.

I sometimes think I should be frightened about dying, but I'm not. I've watched so many go, and find comfort in knowing that I'm to take the same road. If it leads nowhere then that's all right. But if there's a chance of maybe seeing them again, my loved ones, my husband Dinsy and my father and mother and all the rest, then who wouldn't want that? The afterlife, whatever you want to call it, will either be or it won't, and either way I'll be once again with my people, whether that's in heaven or simply down in the same piece of ground.

In our front room, Bill lets himself be drawn up onto my lap, play-acting reluctance, but sensing I suppose my need to have him near. I plant a kiss on his forehead that he scrubs away in exaggerated disgust, first with his hand and then, when the feel of it lingers, with the cuff of his sleeve, keeping up his part in the game but unable to fully hide his smile.

Having him always so close, sharing the days and nights as we do in this house, I can see all the evidence I'll ever need of my blood alive in him, full of all that makes me who I am. Because when I look at him I see all of us reflected, traits of Gina and of Liam, his mother and father, and of the rest of us too – my eyes in a certain light; strains of how my father lifted his head to speak or the delight that would square his shoulders whenever there was a chance to hear a story being told. He has just turned seven, with the best of living still to come, but he's also all of our pasts combined. And because my own future has fallen short, it's the years gone by that shine most clearly for me now.

More than anything, when thinking back, I recall how the light was. Waking slowly, with scarcely the sense that I'd been asleep, to a perfect golden stillness, and lying there among the hot and sweat-soaked sheets, feeling as if someone had dragged me the entire night around the village behind galloping horses. Murmurs of talk lifted now and then from the other side of the bedroom door: Nonie, my aunt, and my sisters, May and poor Annie, who was in her final months already, having been cut asunder by the doctors, breasts first, and then innards, lumps of her, in the chase to catch up with the other thing, the cancer that they'd always known would see her out. Exhausted too from having put down a gruelling night alongside me, their debate now, in low tones, had to do with whether I was in any kind of condition yet to face what couldn't be avoided, or if I should be left to sleep a while longer, since it was clear I needed rest. The morning's brightness, coming through the south-facing window of the St Columba's Terrace room Dinsy and I were renting, our first home as a married couple, lit the wall behind me and spilt over the bed in a way that seemed to deepen the remaining shadow, and from the gloom I reached out my naked arm and spread my fingers to catch a little of its colour. Motes of dust shimmered in a slant of light from the window, and across the road, in the sycamores and horse chestnuts towering above the old high wall of the Protestant graveyard, birds were singing, wrens and sparrows and the slow *tea-cher* notes of the coal tits busy with their games. A morning in April, the sky burning with a trick summer, and I'd been a mother for close to three hours, before Annie, with the others behind her in the doorway, entered the bedroom to tell me otherwise.

'My poor love,' she said, falling short with her effort at a smile, and I just looked at her and sighed because a part of me had known for weeks that something wasn't right. She sat on the edge of the bed, facing me and taking my hand in both of hers, telling me how sorry she was, and I kept gazing out of the window at the treetops and the empty sky until, some minutes later, Nonie brought the baby in, wrapped in an old shawl, a small shape that she placed in my arms so that I could feel the skin, cold as wet rock, against my feverish own. I don't remember if I cried, because it may have been that I'd never stopped, but I do recall kissing him, pressing my lips over and over again to the astonishing details of his face, his forehead and nose and shut eyes and tiny mouth and his chin with the very same cleft that his father had, my one stupid wish for him all the way through my pregnancy, innocent as I was to more important things. His daddy's dimple, a chip off the old block. And still the light poured into the room and the birds continued to sing.

He'd lived for a while, Nonie said, from somewhere in the room. 'A couple of hours, long enough for morning to dawn and longer than he likely should have lasted. But at least he got to know daylight, for how little that matters.' Her words left ruts in me. I'd shed a lot of blood during the delivery, and by the end, after the many hours of labour, couldn't so much as lift my head from the pillow, and if I'd seen him or heard him crying in those initial moments after his birth then all of that was, I'm sorry to say, swallowed by the blackness that overtook me. But what lay in my arms now looked as if it had never known a breath. Life fills up flesh; without it, everything hangs wrong. The shape I held was only what had been left behind of my son, a shell. And yet it was all I had, all *we* had, Dinsy and I. That and the name, John, already chosen in the event of the baby being a boy, at Dinsy's request, after his father, Jack Murphy. I'd dearly wanted Jeremiah, after my own father, and try as I might, couldn't shake the thought that it would be unlucky to name a child for someone who'd died so tragically young – a man whose heart had given out at barely thirty, leaving a helpless widow behind to rear two infants – but in the end, recognising my husband's need, had given way. No photograph had ever existed of Jack Murphy, and neither Dinsy nor his sister retained a single impression of him in their minds, yet his absence from their lives had made a monument of him. For much of my pregnancy, names were the main focus of our conversations, before we decided on John, for a boy, and Mary, if it was a girl, for his mother and for mine, a happy and easy choice. The pair of us lay together in bed night after night, with me feeling safe beside his long frame and his mouth just a light breath away from kissing my cheek, each taking turns at sharing our thoughts and keeping our voices to murmurs though we had no one yet to keep awake, I trying to make him laugh with some of the more outlandish names I could think of, and smiling contentedly at the touch of his large, callused palm resting on my swollen stomach. We'd only recently wed, having been allowed at short notice – grudgingly, given my condition – to the side of the altar, where we'd bowed our heads in shame for the sacrament from the priest, and I was still very much getting used to him. He had ten years on me and I was often caught unawares by the strangeness of his presence in bed, his unexpected touches, and the way his words would come at me in sudden bursts from out of the silence. In spite of that though, I was madly happy. On reflection, I can't say if I was in love yet or merely playing at being, but in some ways it amounted to the same because just living as a grown woman and sharing space with a good man, having to act responsible, was a new and certain thrill. Dinsy's nature, quiet and a little insecure, meant that most of the time I was the one to take charge, but as soon as the lantern was doused and we lay down together our age difference seemed more pronounced. I'd long since let go of the things that made up childhood, but often found myself turning helplessly girlish again. I suppose we're all of us more than one person at a time.

My father always saw me as a girl, too, and I'm not sure that I ever got to be anything else around him, even after I'd given him the grandchildren he'd for so long wanted. The day I announced the news of my first pregnancy to my family, while the others around me wept and shouted about what a disgrace I was, my father remained calm and silent, though I could see the hurt in his eyes, and the disappointment, and when he finally did look at me I was the one who had to look away, hating myself for bringing such trouble to his door. With all his upset, he read my fear and allowed only a few moments of my crying before clearing his throat, telling Annie and May in his usual quiet but solid way that enough was enough, and taking me by the shoulders drew me into a sure embrace. I tried to let him know how sorry I was, and how ashamed, but my words were smothered by the heavy wool of his work-shirt, and I quickly found myself filling up on the taste of it, the combined musk of cigarettes and turf fires and cut grass that in my mind, for no logical reason, was evocative of love. His embrace tightened when he felt my tears seeping through the wool, and he told me in a murmur that it was all right, that this kind of thing happened more often than anyone ever wanted to admit and although I should have known better, and should have listened to all the warnings I'd been given, what was done didn't have to be the end of the world, not any more, not in this day and age.

My recollections have a way of folding in on one another, and that moment of my father's comforting embrace seems connected with the one which found me lying in bed, with my own child's body in my arms, as if they'd occurred on the same day instead of several months apart. I'm inclined to believe that time hangs around me as part of the air, with my purest memories still present in every breath. At any given moment I can close my eyes and find again how I've been at my happiest, or I can find in that same blackness my old ghosts waiting.

To give me this little bit of time, the others, Nonie and my sisters, kept to the bedroom's doorway, and I lay propped up by cushions and coats with John held tightly in my arms, and when I shifted him a little so that he better fit against me, the way the glow of the morning brightened his face intensified my weeping until I could see nothing more than greyness, and I felt as if I was going slowly blind. And then once again Annie was beside me, and May behind her, and I felt hands reaching for the baby and instinctively if only for an instant fought the release. Then, stripped of everything, I squeezed my eyes shut and pressed myself back into the pillow, wanting to die, too.

But of course I didn't die; I merely slept. Fitfully, worn to a nub but with my mind racing, thinking of all I'd done wrong, the sins committed, mistakes made, all the hurt I'd caused, wondering if I was cursed. By early afternoon I'd started to regain something of who I was, but when I tried to lift myself to sit, a vicious rip of pain made me once again faint, and after slumping back down into the pillow my lower parts continued to feel as if they'd been dug out of me, and I knew the wetness between my thighs and beneath me to be blood.

In the time I'd been out, someone had set down a small plate with a slice of bread and margarine on the chair next to the bed, but I couldn't bring myself to eat. Outside, the sky's colour had paled, thinned by a frail skin of cloud, and if the birds still sang then their music was overtaken by the sounds of an ordinary day. We'd all heard the news that, the previous Tuesday, Belfast had been bombed from the air, leaving nearly a thousand dead and as many again injured; but just then, Belfast – and the war, too – seemed a world away from Douglas. And separated from it all, I closed my eyes and once more focused on the pain, the muscles of my body swollen and battered, and my bones prised apart from one another. A hole gaped inside me, and I wondered how it could ever again be filled.

In time I heard the front door opening and the heavy trudge of hobnailed boots on the stairs, and then Dinsy came through into the room. Without opening my eyes I was able to picture him, there at the bedside, afraid and unsure whether to kiss me or reach for my hand. 'Nellie,' he said, and I could hear his breathing, strained from climbing the stairs and coming from the mill at a run, since he only had half an hour for lunch and couldn't be more than a few minutes late back without having his wages docked. And that sound, the slight whistling to his every breath, brought fresh sadness coursing through me and I opened my eyes to find him exactly as I'd imagined: his long, sallow face watching me, his soot-black hair rising up from the top of his head, he having raked his fingers in a worry-gesture through it from forehead to pole. His shirt was open down to the middle of his chest and his sleeves rolled in clumsy fashion up past his elbows, and whatever he saw in my expression caused him to drop onto one knee, awkwardly given his gangly frame, gather up my hand and begin to kiss my knuckles and fingertips. Because he tended the mill's boiler room, the smell of oil on him had become familiar to me, but now I was struck, for the first time and with sudden horror, by just how like the reek of blood it was, mineral, heavy and cloying, and when he leaned in, slipped his hands beneath my arms and raised me up to embrace me – telling me how Nonie had been waiting for him at the door and explained everything, and how sorry he was over it but that it was just life, a tragic fact of it, and we were allowed of course to be sad but we'd still be fine together, that we'd get over this and in the years to come fill a whole house with children – I had a violent urge to push him away. He kissed me and the taste of blood turned my stomach. I knew he was trying to comfort me, but as he crouched there, down on one knee at my side, I also saw how much he was struggling to keep himself together.

'You married me for nothing,' I said when I could, from the deepest and most frightened part of myself, and he looked at me for a long moment, not comprehending at first, before lifting himself back up to his full height.

'That's wrong,' he said. 'And it's not true.'

I turned my face away. 'Isn't it? If I hadn't fallen pregnant, wouldn't I still be living over at home?'

'This is the grief talking, Nellie. I'm the same. Christ, love, I feel like knocking down walls over it. I want to get drunk and never again sober up, and I want to fight the whole village. But what happened happens. It shouldn't and I wish it didn't, but it does. I mightn't say so often enough, and I'm sorry if you didn't know, but the very best thing that ever happened to me was marrying you. And I mean that.'

As meek as I must have looked in the bed, I felt a furnace of anger inside me. I needed reassurance, and to be talked to the way Dinsy was talking now, but a part of me wanted to wallow in my upset, and to be blamed for what had happened. Because I was certain I'd brought

169

all of this on myself, or on us as a couple. I wanted him to be angry with me, to shout at me and weep.

I'd never known Dinsy to be anything but strong. Up and out of the bed every morning before six and into the Mill's stifling boiler room, apart from Sundays when he'd lie in for an hour longer, trying to sleep off the porter he'd put away over in Barrett's the previous night; and never home before the Angelus bell had rung out. Coming in bone-tired then, he'd eat the bit of dinner I had ready for him in a savage, two-handed way, as though food might not cross his plate again for days, before settling down with a newspaper that was often a week past its freshness and which he could barely read. In his happier moments, after coming in from the pub of a Sunday lunchtime to wait out the Holy Hour by devouring a few boiled potatoes crowned with curled scrapings of what butter we could afford, I got to hear his loud rolling laugh, usually while he struggled to recount some ridiculous joke he'd just been told, and the sound of it always made me smile because of how unguarded it seemed, so loose and unexpected, though it confused me somewhat, too, because it succeeded in turning him into a kind of stranger, revealing some layer of him that I'd not yet properly explored. The initial months of our marriage were a dance, I think, having to learn one another's movements and get used to the missteps, and I quickly found myself living for the small revelations that made me realise the man I'd attached myself to wasn't quite, or was often so much more than, who I'd thought him to be. I had wanted to quiver at the sight of him, and for the blood to turn hot in my veins. Instead I found myself tense around him, always ever so slightly braced in anticipation. It wasn't quite fear I felt, but with some of the sense of that. At home, his way was to remain largely silent while I did most of the talking and figured out how to stretch what little money we had left after our rent was paid. Sometimes I watched him when I thought he wasn't looking and saw some of the same tension evident in him, in the stiff way he lifted his shoulders and the slight strain bracketing the corners of his mouth. That was a yielding of sorts, though limited to glimpses, but standing at my bedside now, trying to conceal his pain in a way that only served to lay it bare, he had never seemed so vulnerable.

'I'm sorry, love,' I said. Tall and helpless, keeping himself together ahead of the afternoon's work, he had no response. I wanted him to take me in his arms again, but he didn't. His stare was locked on me but its focus seemed distant, and having kissed me once already I'm not sure it crossed his mind that he might do so again.

Finally, he let out a heavy sigh and said he needed to be getting back to work because they were in the height of trouble with one of the boiler's valves, but that he'd do his best to finish early. He'd speak to Timmy Dorney, the chargehand, about getting someone to cover what was left of the shift. Still he hesitated, though, and it was only when I closed my eyes that he seemed released, and he crossed the room then and, pulling the door quietly shut behind him, muttered some few words that were meant as solace but which I failed to catch.

My father arrived late in the afternoon. When I tried to sit up he waved me back, lifted a timber chair to my bedside from its place in the corner and sat facing me. He had on a collarless shirt and his usual old suit jacket, and when he stooped to kiss my cheek I knew he'd had a couple of drinks – whiskey, given the day that was in it. A slight redness bruised the skin beneath his eyes. I'd never known him to cry, not even when his mother died or when, just a few years later, my brother Jimmy was taken from us too. But there was a wetness about his voice when he spoke that suggested he'd shed a few tears today on my account.

'I've nothing to say about it, Nellie, except how sad it is. Sure, words won't heal you anyway. Nothing will, except time, maybe. But it'll be all right, love. We're most of us who we are because of the things we suffer through.'

'John, his name was.'

'Annie told me. I'm sorry for you, girl. And for Dinsy, too.'

'Did you see him?'

'The baby? I did. A handsome little lad. A bit of a look of your mother, I thought. She always said that with babies we see who we want to see, but why shouldn't the child carry a look of his stock?'

We were always close, my father and I, and that connection had only strengthened in the seven years since cancer took my mother. Maybe it was that we needed now to lean more on one another. I remember from my schooldays how the teacher, Mrs Hanley, in trying to beat the catechism into us, used to tell us that it was a sin to adore anyone but God, but I adored my father and made no apologies for that. He was a man in all things, and he lived for us. I was the youngest, and coming along at a point in his life when he'd already fought his wars and been steeped in so much of the world's horror, I think he sensed in me a certain light. And I was by nature sensitive, in a way that my brothers and sisters, for all their other virtues, were not, which made him protective. I don't mean that I was weak or quiet, but just more sharply attuned to people's feelings and those things left unsaid. Aside from my mother, I believe no one knew my father better than I did, not necessarily the facts of his life as they might be listed on a page but who he truly was as a man. From girlhood, I pleaded with him at every opportunity to tell me about his travels with the army. Some of what he talked about was far-fetched to the point of being downright ridiculous; more still reduced me to a quick mess of tears. But either way, I delighted in what he had to tell, whether of the night, having pulled sentry duty on the Nile after they'd come through the Suez Canal, he saw a mermaid beckoning to him and swimming happily in the water, her long eel-black hair hiding only some of her nakedness and the scales of her great tail shining like pearls in the moonlight; or how he'd once had to spend a week confined to sick bay with a badly dislocated shoulder after rising too sharply from a stoop while passing under the line of the equator; or of the time, in Belgium, he'd seen nuns shot – *mown down*, as he put it – some of them old, others little more than girls, who'd opened their convent as a temporary hospital to patch up and give small comfort to the wounded and the dying, only to be themselves butchered when some enemy company came through. When he talked about these memories, I'd perch on a footstool just opposite him so that we were on either side of the fire, and gaze up into his face; in the same way at five years old as in my twenties and getting myself set to marry, and it was always the seeming devotion of my silence that drew him out, letting him know there was room and stillness enough for him to remember, that he wouldn't be interrupted and could say anything he wanted to without being judged for it. Of course, there was a lot that had to go unspoken, particularly between a father and daughter, but I knew that he said a lot more at that fireside than he ever could have in a confessional, his voice falling so low that at times I had to lean closer to hear, and I looked away whenever I sensed he needed that of me.

Wanting me to rest, Annie had given me just a few minutes before taking John's body. The shawl in which he was coddled was a shade of grey that had started life as black, and she had him so tightly wrapped that I could see nothing but frail wool. And now, listening to my father talk about family resemblances, I realised that I had no image at all in my mind of my baby. The mere mention of my mother let me picture her face very clearly but comparisons were useless. I strained to conjure John in my mind's eye but could conjure nothing that made him mine.

'Nellie?' my father said. 'What is it? What's wrong?'

I tried to speak but at first could only shake my head. He rose a little from his seat, his hand grasping the chair's backrest for support.

'This bed is like a cage,' I said, finally. 'I can't stay here. I need to get up.'

'No, love.' Now he was looming above me. 'Not yet. Give yourself a day or two. It'll be time enough then and you'll feel the better for it.'

I ignored him, pulled the blankets back from the other side of the bed, moved my bare feet over the edge of the mattress and tried to raise myself to a sitting position. Instantly, a shock of pain tore through me, jarring a high-noted cry from my chest. The urge to lie back down was immense, but I clenched my eyes shut and counted seconds until my body adjusted itself to its new position. When I could, I let my toes find the floor, and moved forward inch by inch until I trusted my legs to bear the weight.

'Can't you stay put, Nellie?' my father said, but he came around the bed and held me by the elbows in support. 'The rest will do you good.'

I looked up at him and shook my head. 'I'm going with you,' I told him, almost spitting the words, needing them said. 'You didn't rear a fool, Dad. I don't need to be told what will happen now. You're waiting for Dinsy, and ye won't go until late but it has to be tonight. And I'm going, too.'

He repeated my name, in a pleading way, but made no further answer, and the silence began to yawn between us.

'Don't take that from me, Dad,' I said. 'And don't ask me to just accept what you wouldn't stand for, yourself.'

His eyes were shining and I was struck, as I'd been so often, by his scale and strength, his chest and shoulders like the trunk of an oak, that broad and strong. Built to endure, and to shield and shelter us all. Middle age was turning old on him, but his core was not yet for crumbling.

'You'd be better off staying put,' he told me, still trying to do right, and turned his face towards the window. The first strains of dusk were closing in but we'd already reached that part of the year when the days were beginning to stretch, and so night, the cover of which was essential for what needed to be done, remained a way off yet. 'Or if you won't stay here, I'll take you over home so that May can make a fuss of you. Seeing what has to be done will do you no good at all, love. Dinsy and I can handle things.' But I knew by his tone that he'd already in his heart given way to me. Most likely, he could see that there was no sense in an argument.

I tried to stand but it didn't take. When he saw that I was about to fall he took my weight and guided me around the foot of the bed, found my clothes, which were folded over the back of a chair, sat me down carefully and helped me to dress. Privacy didn't matter; for these few minutes he was me and I him, and as I raised my hands above my head the way I used to as a little girl, he moved with ease about me, peeling me out of my nightgown, slipping on the loose vest, my blouse and then, after he'd paused to give me a moment's rest, my pinafore.

For the better part of a decade following his return from the war, he'd been friendly with a nun, a woman from Clare who was based for a few years in Cork but who he had met in France while he was being passed through one of the field hospitals. Sister Bríd. I was only a young child and saw her no more than three or four times, but I do recollect that she was disfigured down the left side of her face, blind in that eye and with skin like turned earth and a mouth that hung as if snagged on a briar. She seemed afraid of everything and everyone, but could laugh and felt for some reason comfortable with him. The convent had her working as a nurse in the North Infirmary, and every couple of weeks her shift rotated to night duty, and because that was, for reasons I couldn't have imagined, a cause of enormous upset to her, my father – I think more in a gesture of companionship and reassurance than for any actual assistance he could lend – would go and help with her rounds.

I remember a day when my mother, generally such a quiet, easy-going sort, got on at him, wanting to know why he was putting himself to such trouble. She knew well enough that this other woman was no threat, so her complaint wasn't fuelled by jealousy, and she tried to temper her words so they sounded more hurt than angry, but couldn't help feeling a bit put out by the fact that he had someone else in his life outside his family and was spending these nights away from us, away from her. As young as I was, I saw the disappointment in his expression, but he didn't interrupt while my mother unburdened her frustrations and insecurities. Once she'd finished saying her piece he told her that he was helping out because he'd been asked to, by someone who wouldn't have asked anything lightly, of him or anyone else. And, he said, he'd found himself good with the sick and wounded, that out of necessity, in the trenches of France and Flanders, he'd helped nurse his share and more besides, and being one of the lucky ones to have made it home he felt he owed that little bit of himself, these few hours a couple of times a month, because others had given plenty more and paid a far higher cost. My mother cried to hear him talk in so forthright a way, he simply explaining how he felt rather than trying to confront or chastise, accepting as he did that she could never fully relate to what he was talking about, that no one could who hadn't been through it. I knew she felt ashamed then of the thoughts that had filled her head, and it was for this reason, I'm sure, that quarrels rarely lasted long between them and making up was always so easy.

With me, now, he had the same gentle way about him, and I got to see the same caring side of him that had tended to the wounded in those trenches and the consumptive here in Cork. He helped me dress and when I started to cry pressed his lips to my cheek and assured me that with a bit of time I'd get over this, and I'd have many good and happy days ahead of me yet, me and Dinsy, both. Wishing that his words could possibly be true, I laughed through my tears at him, slipped my bare feet into the sandals he'd set in place before me, and once again got unsteadily to my feet.

At Forge View, the wait until midnight felt interminable. Annie had the fire lit, and though none of us were cold we sat around it, me in my father's chair, May and Annie sharing the second seat across from me. Dinsy and my father lingered for a while out in the yard with my brother, Dixie, who'd stopped in on his way home from work, the three of them talking only in snatches, more comfortable in silence than in words.

As a way of passing the time we drank cocoa, cups of the stuff, the milk warmed in a billycan hung over the fire, then filled mugs with porter for the men from a large copper jug. Dinsy downed his as it was, cold and capped with froth from having sat some days in the cottage's lean-to pantry, but my father moved in close by the fire, laid the poker a while among the embers then plunged the glowing iron tip of it into his drink. The hiss of the hot iron mulling the black liquor seemed as loud in the room as a leaving train and reminded me of all the Christmas nights that I'd known this done, and I smiled to see the mug give up a small cough of steam visible only because of the firelight.

John wasn't the first of our family's infants to die. Dixie and his wife had been a couple of times through similar, a stillborn girl late in the first year of their marriage and then, again, after their first child that lived, another girl who'd survived a week or so after being born small and early. She'd at least been christened, though; there'd been time for that, if only just, which made a difference.

I tried to keep my eyes fixed to the fire, the different colours of the flames as they ate traces of turf bricks above the long-burning cinders, but I was all the time aware of the bedroom door, not ten feet off to my left and pulled shut in a way that, through the entirety of my life, it had almost never been. Six children including me had been born within the walls of that room, and three people had drawn their final breath – my poor brother, Jimmy; my mother; and my father's mother, who'd returned from England when I was little to die surrounded by those she loved and in the place where she'd been at her happiest. Now my baby waited there, alone in the room's silence, laid in an open plywood box that had been hastily nailed together late this afternoon out of scrap timber salvaged from the forge across the road.

The night deepened and we all began to feel caught in a kind of limbo, at once yearning for this day to be over but at the same time, because of what we were about to do, afraid of what the new one might bring.

'What time is it, at all?'

I leaned forwards in the chair and peered at the clock on the mantle. Years of scorching had stained the glass, almost obscuring the face.

I turned back to Dinsy.

'Just gone eleven, I think, love.' The ticking had such stiff monotony that anything more than a few minutes of exposure turned you deaf to it, but now that I'd become aware of it again the sound seemed once more slow and very loud.

'That's late enough, I'd say.' He cleared his throat but his voice remained distant. 'What do you think, Jer?'

My father said he thought it was, that there wouldn't be many roaming the Churchyard Lane at this hour. The corner of the room that he'd taken up had him entirely swallowed, and I could make out only the outline of him until he caught a little of the fire's light. In response to his movement, I raised myself from the chair. I could feel my sisters watching me and knew they had the same thing in their minds to say, but neither of them did, since I was past the point of reason. In getting so abruptly to my feet I had to brace myself against the flare of heat that once again shuddered through me, and while nobody else noticed, I think my father sensed it because he stepped quickly close, gave me his arm and let me link him, and I was grateful for his strength but also afraid because the feeling of faintness was slow this time to pass. Behind us, Dinsy cleared his throat again as if to speak, but when no words came he went through into the bedroom and emerged a minute or two later with the small wooden box cradled in both arms against his chest. My father and I moved back to give him space, then followed him outside onto the road.

Two shovels had been placed just inside our front wall earlier, and my father took one while Dinsy shifted the box a little, light as it must have been, to set his left hand free, and picked up the other. Then we started off through the Hall Field and out onto the New Road. We moved with care, and in silence so as not to disturb the late hour and because we were each of us locked in our own thoughts, I feeling small but secure in between my two men.

Once out in the open, we stopped to consider our situation. The sky, clear as glass for most of the day, had clouded over, which lent the darkness a sinister heft, the three-quarter moon blocked out. Tonight, though, this was the sky we wanted. And we knew the way well enough without the need of either moon or starlight to guide us.

An old wall separated the road from the hallowed ground. It wasn't particularly high on our side, reaching roughly to my chin, but dropped a dozen feet or more down into the graveyard.

'How should we do this?' Dinsy asked.

There were two ways around to the cemetery's front gate: either by following the road back down into the village and along by St Columba's Terrace, where Dinsy and I lived and where we'd be as likely as not seen, even at this late hour; or by going the opposite way, off to our left, up and over the Bow Wow Bridge and down the Chapel Steps, which meant having to pass the church and, worse, the rectory, with its enormous wolfhound penned in to the front garden, a beast with a bark fit to bring the longest-planted bodies back up out of the ground. Either choice, especially making allowance for how slowly I could move, put a further ten or fifteen minutes of walking on us.

My father leaned against the wall. Hundreds of disordered grave markers jutted pale and ugly as crooked teeth from the blackness, yet I could have picked out our small plot blindfolded and without a moment's hesitation. Tucked in under an old forwards-tipping hawthorn, ground already packed with the bones of my grandmother, my mother and my brother.

'Let you climb in and get started, lad, and Nellie and I will make our way around to the gate. That way we won't be carrying anything if we're seen. It'll just look like I'm seeing her home.'

Dinsy muttered something in agreement, pressed the small coffin into Jer's arms, then gripped the top of the wall and set about hoisting himself up and over. But before he could get away I took hold of his coat sleeve.

'Wait.' I looked up at him, then back at my father. 'I don't want us separating. We can all go in this way.'

'You're in no fit state to be climbing walls, Nellie.'

'You're not, girl,' my father agreed. 'You'll do yourself damage.'

'I won't,' I said, having already, and really just in that moment, made up my mind. 'Down towards the corner there, the drop's a bit lower. Let you go in ahead of us, Dad. Dinsy will get me up on the wall and then lower me down to you. We'll go easy, and I'll be all right. But it's better this way. We won't risk being seen, and it'll save me the walk.'

The work, digging out the foot of the grave to a depth of a yard or more, was gruelling, especially given the lateness of the hour and the need for relative quiet. Despite the falling temperatures, Dinsy stripped down to his vest and my father to his shirtsleeves, for the freedom of movement and because they knew from experience – my father, especially – just how quickly their exertions would have them sweating. They took up a position either side of the grave and set to the task, staggering their shovelling in some effort at a back-and-forth rhythm, both of them conscious of the need to pace themselves and yet keen, also, to get finished. I tucked myself in beneath the hawthorn and watched, glad of the branches above and all around me laden with blossom, a pink summer-smelling fur that retained its vibrancy even in the darkness, and when I grew sore from being on my feet, I lowered myself and sat with my back against the tree's trunk, embracing John's body. Apart from the digging sounds the night was coldly silent, but after some time had passed I began to hear the rattling of my father's increasingly laboured breath, a kind of tail-end whine to every exhalation. Before I had a chance to speak up, my husband, who'd also noticed, sank the blade of his shovel into the earth with a stamp of his boot heel, and straightened up slowly, in a way that forced my father to stop, too.

'Christ,' Dinsy gasped, acting more beaten than he was. 'This really knocks it out of a fella.'

My father set his hands over the shovel's handle and drew it back against his chest. He knew what Dinsy was doing but left it go unchallenged and concentrated on taking air until his breathing lost its harshness. Then, once again, they set themselves to the task of digging.

None of us heard the priest until he was almost upon us. Later on, I'd blame myself for that, because the others had their work as an excuse. But because the night in that graveyard was such an absolute, and because of how long and harrowing the day had been, I was struggling to keep my eyes open. That shamed me, too, being so weak against the drag of sleep when, barely an arm's reach away, my father and husband were sweating to dig my son's grave, and I had his boxed-up corpse across my lap.

Dinsy was the first to lift his head, in response to the small scrape of a footstep on the loose gravel path somewhere behind me. He reached out and caught my father's arm, and I sat a little forwards, and after some seconds we heard it again, then repetitions of it, loud now and drawing close, the unmistakable crunching of shoe heels, clear, unhurried and making no effort at all at stealth.

We didn't move because there was no escape, nowhere to run to or hide. And in a situation like this, I knew that neither Dinsy nor my father were the running kind.

The steps approached and after some seconds the priest appeared from between the graves. Father Field was a wide, round-chested man, as tall as the two he faced now but decked out in such blackness that his face, pale by comparison, seemed disembodied, and his hand too, when he raised it and did something with his fingers, a kind of fluttering gesture, oddly effeminate, the meaning of which, whether intended as greeting or threat, was lost on us.

'What's going on here?' he asked, sounding more curious than offended, as if he'd simply stumbled across us while out enjoying a casual stroll, his voice caught in an unusually high pitch, lacking the bottom that the safe echoes of the pulpit usually lent it. We stared back at him, but no one spoke while he considered each of us in turn, his gaze falling lastly on me but not lingering. Then my father, some five or six feet away, began to clean the blade of his shovel with the heel of his boot.

'What do you want, Father?' he asked.

'Jer, isn't it? Jer Martin?'

'That's right.'

'What are you doing out here, this time of night, Jer? Haven't ye homes to go to?'

I could hear my father's breathing again, not tight from the work now but from trying to remain calm.

'You think this is funny?'

He spoke in such a way that the instinct of the priest, uncertain of having heard correctly, was to take a short step closer.

'Funny?' The priest seemed confused. 'What do you mean?'

'I mean, the smirk. The laugh in your voice.'

We'd been caught, and I was trembling. But now a deeper dread stirred in me, not just because of what my father was saying but by his measured tone. I leaned my weight sideways onto my right arm and turned my head away from the priest, certain that I was going to vomit. Dinsy dropped his shovel and came to kneel beside me.

'I know what you're doing,' the priest said, speaking generally rather than to any one of us, having recovered his authority and trying to make a shield of it by letting his voice broaden. 'You've no business here. You're trespassing. You're all trespassing.'

My father had the shovel crossways, the restless shuffling of his fingers the only compromise to his stillness. As thoroughly as I thought I'd known him in talk, for the first time in my life I caught a hint of the soldier he must once have been. 'No,' he said, without raising his voice or looking away. 'We're not. This piece of ground belongs to us, and don't anyone dare try and tell me different. My dead are buried here, my wife, my mother, my sister and my child. And what we're at is none of the Church's business. Not tonight.'

'Jer Martin,' the priest said again, loudly, as if making a note of the name. But his bluster now was growing thin, and I could sense his fear and knew that it was not misplaced. 'I'll read you from the altar, and I'll have the guards at your door in the morning. Christ almighty, man, you're a long way from the first to try this. Do you honestly think we've not had men come in here over the years, looking to bury their bastards?'

The shovel raised and readied itself in my father's hands. 'Call me what you like in your church,' he said, his tone dropping a notch and sounding worse for it. 'Sure, that's all you're fit for. But just chance saying that word to me once more and, so help me, I'll put a smirk on your mouth that you'll never be able to drop.'

At that, Dinsy moved from my side as if to intercede, but my father put him back on his heels with a sideways glance. 'No, lad. It needs saying. These priests think they're kings, but the worst of them should be put up against a wall and shot for the pain they cause people.'

'You're making a mistake.' Father Field tried laughing again. 'You all are. A big mistake. And you'll be sorry for it.'

Except for the breeze stirring the hawthorn above me, I might have believed the world had stopped turning, until my father spoke again.

'I've known your kind my whole life,' he told the priest. 'Set the guards on me if you have to. I'll take what comes. But, this minute, you have a choice to make. You can turn around and walk away, get yourself back home and into bed or go and say whatever prayers you think need saying. Or you can stay here and see what happens. Because there's room enough in this ground for one more. And if you know me at all then you'll know I'll not hesitate.'

'You're mad,' the priest said, and repeated himself in a shout, as if we were a field away instead of mere paces. He took a long step backwards and then another and, in his haste to get out again onto the path, stumbled on the rugged ground and retained his footing only after colliding against the corner of a tilting headstone. And with the gravel crunching once more beneath his feet and taking courage from the increased distance between him and us, he stopped a moment and repeated that we were making a big mistake, all of us, that we'd burn in hell for what we were at, desecrating his cemetery with our filthy, mortal sin. From where I sat I could no longer see him, yet when my father raised the shovel again as if threatening a blow I was able to picture his reaction, the sudden violence of his flinch, and within seconds this vision seemed borne out by the sound of his hurried, panicked retreat.

None of us spoke. The sound of the footsteps grew faint, the small turnstile gate groaned open and shut, and my father returned to his position at the graveside and slammed the blade of his shovel back down into the ground. Dinsy picked up his own shovel and moved into place opposite, no longer having to worry about the noise. And when they'd reached a depth that made tandem digging awkward and there was only room for one man at a time in the hole, they took turns, again without a word of discussion, switching every five or ten minutes, one going in while the other leaned against the shaft of the shovel and looked on, neither of them really resting, their faces – from what I was able to make out – harried and full of fury. Then at last my father, shoulders-deep in the ground, straightened up, and set a hand into the small of his back.

'That's down far enough, would you think, Dinsy?'

'I'd say it is, yeah.'

He took the shovel from my father, then helped him from the hole. I set the box down on the grass and struggled to my feet. After sitting for so long, pain hacked at me in a dozen places, and as I reached for the tree to steady myself, I was overcome with a deep and certain dread that my insides would at any second spill out of me onto the ground at my feet. For the men's sake, I was glad it was still dark.

'Are you all right, love?'

I closed my eyes and felt as if I was being spun.

'Grand,' I said, biting back a sob. 'A stitch, that's all. I just moved too sudden. It'll pass in a minute.'

To distract myself, I focused on Dinsy, who'd come around the grave and was lifting the box from the ground.

And as I watched, he did something entirely unexpected: he wiped his hands roughly on the seat of his trousers, picked apart John's covering shawl and, very gently, until he was overcome by a strangling of tears, kissed our baby's cheeks and forehead.

'We'd better get on,' my father said. Murmuring the words, not directing them to either of us, but needing them spoken and knowing that we did, too. 'It starts getting bright early, these mornings.' He hesitated, and again cleared his throat. 'It's time, I'd say.'

Dinsy pinched away the tears from his eyes, looked at us as if only just hearing, and nodded, then with great care pulled the shawl once more across our child's face. Whatever happened for us moving forward, I knew I'd keep as something precious this glimpse of him. The side that, in trying to be strong and not quite making it, he'd for the first time let me fully see. The revelation that his heart really could be hurt just as thoroughly as my own changed something between us, I think.

With the coffin in his arms, he climbed into the grave and laid our baby down. I came out from under the hawthorn and looked on as he gripped my father's hand and let himself be hauled back out into the world. We huddled together then, the three of us, just as before but no longer quite the same, feeling permanently lessened. And when, because no one was saying anything, I asked if there was need for a prayer, my father sighed and said that I should go ahead and say one if I wanted and if I thought it would make me feel better, but that in his mind if any god was listening, one that cared a damn for us, then silence would be heard just as well as any words. I shivered and Dinsy, having no coat to wrap around me, put his arm across my shoulders, and my father took my hand in his, and we remained like that for some time, not moving, thinking our own thoughts and staring into the opened ground, letting the silence, just as he'd suggested, be our prayer.

'Let you take Nellie home, Dinsy.' My father's voice, when it came, was like a husk scraped clean. 'I can finish up here. Ye look beat, the pair of ye.'

'No,' I said, without lifting my head, stubborn to the last. 'I'm not going. Not unless we all go.'

What he'd said was right; Dinsy and I were done in. I remained upright, somehow, but could only draw breath in sighs and didn't want to think about having to walk. The few minutes' distance to our tenement room, and as long again to Forge View, seemed impossibly far.

Dinsy picked up the shovels and passed one to my father. 'We'll stay,' he said. 'Sure, it's not worth our while going now.' And as he turned away from me and plunged his shovel into the mound of displaced soil I noticed that the moon had finally fallen into view – a fragment of it the shining colour of buttermilk – as well as a few flecks of starlight, in a clear patch of sky above us. Its glow lit his back, the sweat-lacquered skin of his shoulders rounded heavy from all the weight of the day and night. He tossed the first load of earth down into the hole and the heavy thump of it hitting the grave's bottom couldn't take from the more muted sound of what spillage connected with the shrouded body. A second shovelful was a nearly exact echo, and this time as he turned back towards the mound I heard him sobbing, a terrible grunt of tears. I envied him that release and felt my own shame deepen, because he was seeing in his mind what I was seeing, which was all there was, our baby lying beneath a rain of earth, and yet he could cry and I, in this most anguished of moments, could not.

The only hope we had now was to finish this quickly, but for what seemed like a long time the grave continued to gape, its blackness a chasm that the moonlight couldn't penetrate. The men kept on, and the loud, heavy sound of the shovelfuls of dirt gradually lightened and the hole grew shallow.

If we hadn't already been found out, we'd have had to carefully flatten the earth so that Paddy Reilly, the cemetery's gravedigger, wouldn't notice that the grave had been opened. Such precautions now seemed unnecessary, yet my father insisted on spreading the last of the leftover soil as smoothly as he could, not for the benefit of any who might scrutinise the ground for signs of interference but because this was our grave, and he wanted it to look right.

We started back for my father's house, avoiding the heart of the village by following the road past the parochial house and the church, then over the lane towards the Finger Post and back along by the forge. In choosing this route, not only were we less likely to be seen, we also knew that those who did happen to spot us from the few houses we'd pass would keep talk of it among themselves.

Dinsy led the way through the graveyard, his shovel like a rifle against his right shoulder, the head of it fanning the air behind him, up along the narrow gravel path with headstones tipping towards us and away on either side, to the same barrel-gate that the priest had taken in escaping us a couple of hours before. The hinges squealed as I passed through, causing me to shudder. While we'd been within its walls, the graveyard had seemed nothing more than a field of grass and rocks. But now, just as we were getting out, the dead felt on the rise. At that small, witchy hour, it was as if the whole wide world and all of its beyond was watching.

'We'll get a drop of rain before it turns properly light, I reckon,' my father said. 'And after that the ground will look like it's never been touched.'

I tightened my grip on his arm.

'What do you think will happen with Father Field?'

'Him? Nothing. He'll know better than to kick up. Don't be worrying about that.'

Our slow pace dropped still further as we approached the rectory and braced ourselves for the thunder of the wolfhound's arrival at the garden's front wall. But for once the animal wasn't to be seen, and without questioning his absence and not wanting to push this one small piece of good fortune too far, we hurried by and tried to put as much quick distance as we could between us and our problems.

'But he'll have to respond,' Dinsy said, once we were past the church, and clear. 'Don't you think? I mean, he'll lose a lot of face otherwise.' Talking just for the sound of the words, I knew; that being a way of his at certain times. Either a glut of words or silence. He had just buried our baby, but speaking of the priest was easier than having to face the fact of our devastation.

'He won't talk,' my father said. 'And he knows we won't either. It'd be as bad for him as for us if it were to come out. He might have a word with the Sergeant, just to throw a scare into me. But he'll know it won't be in his interest to go shouting about it, whatever he feels. The Church might still rule the roost, but he was right when he said we're not the first to have done what we've done.'

'So you think this'll be the end of it?'

'I do, lad. He'll leave a few days pass, and then I'll open the door some morning and he'll be there, waiting. He'll let on, without saying it in so many words, that he's well acquainted with what grief can do to people, and I'll nod my head and act contrite, because he'll want to see that I still know my place. And as he's leaving he'll mention something about the missions, angling for a small contribution. And we'll both know that my few pennies can expect to make it no further than the snug of Two-Bob Barrett's.'

I put the time at somewhere after three o'clock, but none of us was carrying a watch and nothing about the sky hinted at when dawn might begin to shift the night. The prospect of my father's predicted rain felt more wishful than likely, but I supposed it didn't matter much if there was going to be any truth at all in the rest of what he'd said. By now I'd grown numb to the worst of my pain but every forty or fifty paces I needed to stop for a minute, to press my fingers in between my thighs, needing that support against the sense that my insides were collapsing.

On either side of me the men waited, and tried to act distracted by how the stars were lighting up the increasingly bare patches of sky or the stillness of the road with, up ahead of us, the enormous and ancient horse chestnut trees frozen into silence now that the breeze had fallen away. Eventually we reached those trees, and the old ivy-coated wall that hemmed them in, and with each advancing step the Finger Post rose higher into view, like a ship's mast coming up from behind the horizon, pressing itself into the sky; how joyous a sight I imagined that must have been for those who found themselves stranded and in need of saving. Our high crossroads signpost promised salvation of a kind too, the first hint of it, enough to lift my heart and pour a modicum of strength into me, signalling as it did that we were very nearly home. Our pace didn't quicken, but I could feel my father's and Dinsy's relief, too, at the thought of having familiar walls around us once again.

I hadn't realised how cold I was until I entered the cottage and was folded into the room's heat. May, who'd waited up and kept the fire going, led me to the armchair. Apart from the small resistance of the flames, the room was dark. I sat back in the chair and the world came down on me, making it difficult to think. Dinsy left the shovels propped against the wall outside, and last to enter, came to the fire rubbing his hands together. His skin jaundiced by the light from the flames, the lines of his face stacked with shadows, he didn't turn his head when Annie arrived between us and pressed a glass into his hand and another into mine.

That was the first time I tasted whiskey. Now, some four decades later at the age of sixty-four, I find myself sitting with glass again in hand, this time a long splash of Powers with two heaped teaspoons of sugar to balance the bitterness of two mashed painkilling pills. I am still less than a hundred feet from my father's old front door, albeit in a council house, one in a square of twenty-eight filling up the field ahead of the estuary in a way that would have been unimaginable to me when I was a girl. Our house backs onto the main road, next door to what used to be, in my childhood, the forge, a long-lost trade that first came into being on the side of our road a century before my time, but is now a small, musky, wool-smelling shop selling carpets for floors no longer made of dirt. And now, out of those who'd huddled close to the fire with me on that long-ago sombre night, only May remains, she – like me – years widowed, but still here, still at home in Forge View, a name that needs explaining now for strangers and the young, but everything about it, apart from the piped water and the electric light, unchanged.

There's not a day goes by that May and I don't visit one another, though for the past couple of years, since my time has started falling away, it's been she who usually crosses over the road to me. She is six years older than me, which puts her at seventy, but though she is beginning to wear her age, somehow I'm the one that time has beaten. Our door is always on the latch, and even if I am dozing I will recognise the slight fall of her footsteps. She takes up the armchair and we chat, keeping our gossip small and letting ourselves reminisce.

I'm having trouble keeping down food, and I know what everyone's been thinking and, I suppose, waiting for. But being as close as we are, May and I can be easy together in silence as we watch over my grandson, Bill. School hasn't yet tamed him and at this stage likely won't, and he's always picking at something he should be leaving alone and up to devilment of some sort: climbing on the backs of the chairs and leaping onto the windowsill; trying to throw small things into the fire – pieces of newspaper, twigs or leaves that he has collected from the garden – for the simple excitement of watching them burn; or using the fireplace's kerb as a circus high-wire that he inches along, tottering from one corner to the other in his uncertain and dramatic heel-to-toe fashion. May, such a sweet soul but never having had children of her own, is often blue in the face from chastising him and pleading with him for the love of Christ above in heaven to be careful, to get down off the sideboard or to not be sliding down the stairs head first and on the flat of his back, telling him about the boy in Rochestown – made up, of course – who snapped his neck doing that, or the girl from up in Scairt who hung herself a few years back on the strings of the venetian blinds while trying to play Tarzan. That's his usual self, but just recently I've noticed Bill more muted. Either his mother, my Gina, has been talking to him or else he's read the atmosphere of the house, sensing that something is the matter, without knowing quite what. And now, in the front room, with the wind humming in the chimney, he lies stretched out on his stomach on the cold linoleum between our feet, playing his games of war, talking to himself in frenzied murmurs and with his few toy soldiers alive against his little fingers, and May and I recognise and feel a kind of shared sadness over how unnatural a state this is for him, how good he is trying to be without having to be told.

There are no beginnings, my father once told me, and no ends. It had been his experience, he said, that until our hearts stop beating, there's only what lies between, and that's a time of war and nothing but. I often ponder this, and I believe I know what he meant, though I'd struggle to explain the thought in a way that makes sense. You need to have felt it. For the past week or so my mind has been full of a day, back in '63, when Dinsy came in after a long shift of work, looking wan and tired, and because the bit of dinner wasn't quite ready decided he'd lie down on our bed and close his eyes for half an hour. He'd left both the front door and the door to the bedroom wide open, the only way we had of getting air into the place, and from where I was, busily buttering slices of bread in the pantry that he'd put up a couple of summers prior, I could hear the creak of the bed's springs when he sat to untie his boots and then again, with greater emphasis, when he lay down. For the couple of minutes that followed his breathing seemed very loud in the otherwise silent house, and then suddenly it changed, grew clotted, as if he were sucking air through a piece of sackcloth. Because I'd lived so long with his noises I instantly felt this difference, the wrongness of it, and I threw down what was in my hands and, already too late, ran through to him. Almost immediately Gina, who'd been in the chair by the window trying to puzzle her way through some confusion of maths homework, was beside me, swept along by my panic, and not knowing what else to do I threw myself to my knees, grabbed Dinsy's face with both my hands and began to cry out his name. Trying to wake him, unable to accept the facts, or refusing to, until eventually, either because my howls had been overheard or because Gina had run outside for help, one of our neighbours from across the road was lifting me to my feet, pulling me into her arms and telling me that I needed to stop, that the young one was in the doorway, watching, seeing everything. It's all there in my mind, startling in its clarity, a scene plucked at random from a film in which I am the camera. I know that, in the minutes after, other neighbours arrived too, men as well as women, crowding into the small house. But all of that is a blur because with Dinsy gone, the present, such as it was, felt stripped of its essential colours.

Maybe there's some truth to the notion of time's healing qualities, but there's also no denying that life occasionally breaks in ways that can't be mended. We watch and wait and squeeze the hands of our dying, trying to comfort them when there's nothing left to say, and then we put them in the ground, weep a while for them and for ourselves. And when enough time has passed – because we have no other choice – we search among the fragments of whatever remains to us for a reason to keep moving forwards, then we step back into a world that, indifferent to our tribulations, has continued all the while to turn, and we go on breathing until our own air runs out. There's no real getting over those kinds of losses, the death of a spouse or a child, but they must be borne. And, of course, the losses I've endured are not unique.

Forge View, my childhood family home, perches at the side of what has become a very busy road, a two-lane track of tarmacadam now rather than gravel, but otherwise just as it always was, from the time of its initial laying, set down with coach horses in mind. That home saw all of us into the world and more than a few of us buried but never actually belonged to our family, and the rent still costs May a tidy piece of her pension, money she has to count out on a weekly basis to Two-Bob Barrett, the publican occupying the near corner of the East village. The Barrett family claimed ownership of Forge View a long time back, as they did with other houses and patches of ground that weren't bound by deeds, they being people educated about such things and with the right connections in the County Hall. I don't have to be there to see how it plays, because I've accompanied her often enough down through the years and witnessed for myself the way Two-Bob leans back against the wall behind the bar, his stick-like arms folded across his chest, acting casual but watching while May tallies up her fist of coins and paper notes, taking close measure of the slow count, his mouth chewing a patient smirk, part of him delighting in how the men sitting at the counter with their pints of stout at that lunchtime hour have no choice but to see, too, though most of them try for my sister's sake to pretend otherwise.

Still, no matter whose name hangs over the cottage, the air within Forge View these days is entirely May's, the mood of the place slow and musty, spiced with bygone moments, and the walls themselves know who belongs within and who does not. Sitting, listening to the clock make slices of the days, May keeps all her ghosts close, and a week rarely passes, she told me once, that she doesn't hear something, the murmur of children's laughter or older voices hushed in conversation in the next room, and whether that has to do with spectres or is merely her mind unfurling spent moments is of no consequence, she says, because that's surely what hauntings are.

As close as May and I were to our parents, Gina is to me. Talking to her is like thinking out loud, we've become that much a part of one another. She was the one I leaned on most heavily in those first years after Dinsy's death, and who gave me the most of herself, more than I probably should have taken. And I've become a burden again now that I am in need of nursing, though she has enough to do trying to cope with Bill and Martin. She'd argue such a notion away because she never wants to hurt anyone's feelings, even if it means setting her own aside, but I see the strain of it in her face, and the forlorn train that her thoughts tend to follow.

'Can't you see a doctor?' she pleaded, on one of those mornings when the sight of me became too much for her. I was sitting in the front room in my vest, trying to wash from a dish of warm soapy water, and had all the look of a scarecrow after a month of gales.

'No doctor,' I said, as runnels of water trickled down my neck and gathered in the hollows of my collarbones. 'I see enough of him as it is. More of him than I'd like, if it was up to me. Sure, isn't he here nearly every second day now.'

'Not Brett, Mam. I mean a specialist. Someone that knows about this, and can maybe do something for you.'

As she spoke she was grinding my painkillers into powder. She gives me my pills with whiskey, two every morning and two more at night, which is already double what has been instructed, but when I start to believe my end is near she increases my dose by as much again, crushing them carefully between two tablespoons, half a pill at a time, so that nothing is lost. I know she'd give me the whole bottle of pills, if I asked it of her.

'I'm not talking about hospital,' she said. 'I just want you to get a bit of relief.'

'Brett's as good as the next quack,' I told her, shaking my head at how little such words mattered any more. 'And sure, don't I have his tablets? What else can the man give me? If I allow him half a chance, he'll start on about them opening me up. Just for a look, just to see what's going on. But they did that with Annie, and it was the finish of her. No, love, I'm grand where I am. I'm in my own house, with my family all around me. How could anyone hope for more than that? But if you don't mind, I might lie down a while, and maybe get an hour or two. I didn't sleep a wink all night, and I've a fierce tiredness over me.'

Until recently I used to sleep upstairs, and make it back down of a morning by sitting and shuffling forward, step by slow, jolting step. But one day my daughter's husband Liam intervened, insisting that it wasn't right, me trying to rest a long day on the couch, and he took my bed asunder and set it up here in the front room, just beside the window.

Gina considered me for some length of time. The worry was clear in her face, and her eyes, the same cold blue as my own, looked to have grown very small. Finally, she hitched her shoulders in a surrendering shrug and went to the kitchen to boil the kettle, returning a few minutes later with a pink hot-water bottle wrapped in a tea towel. Better than any nurse, she helped me into bed and laid me down on my side, then put a pillow beneath my head and the hot-water bottle to the mid-point of my back, precisely where I needed it. I gasped at its sudden heat and waited for the burning to abate, and then I closed my eyes. The wireless on the sideboard was tuned to Radio Éireann, with the volume kept low, a stream of talk interrupted only now and then by music, new-sounding stuff to my ears but which is already considered old, and I don't mind the rock-and-roll but I prefer the ballads. Before we made it to the hourly headlines I was dozing, but even in sleep I heard Gina flitting about the place, getting down on her knees to scrape with the hand-shovel beneath the fire's grate, and then the hush of the ash and cinders as she piled them onto sheets of newspaper, and the crackle of the new fire laid of turf and kindling, and a few knobs of coal. That or, from the kitchen, the noise of her filling the kettle for tea, and feeding Bill cornflakes or a slice of toast, talking to him all the while in murmurs, trying as best she could to keep the house quiet both for my sake and Liam's, who had not long come in off a twelve-hour night shift and was upstairs, tossing and turning in his own bed.

This is the only kind of sleep I get now. Noises don't bother me; I rest better by day than by night, knowing I have others near. I expect that when my time comes I'll simply slip away, but the one upsetting thought I have is of being alone when it happens, of going in the middle of the night, with everything in darkness. I'm not looking for prayers, or for tears, but having a loved one there will let me feel that my life has in some way mattered, and that I'm not just another leaf stripped from a tree by some October gale. My eyes are closed, but my mind is always full, and I don't think I ever truly lose consciousness any more. I keep the world close around me, the murmuring of the wireless, the movements in the house, and this strange slumber of mine streams with recollections, with faces I see every day and others I've not looked on in half a lifetime, but each as alive and real as the other. My mother is here a lot now, more and more it seems, quiet as she always was, but smiling, and my father, too, the pair of them as they'd been when I was a girl of nine or ten and still most in need of them, and I wonder sometimes if seeing them so often has meaning, if there's a sign in it, but when the pills I've taken start to wear off and the pain seeps through again I'm not able to care so much about what lies ahead. While I have a window to look out of I don't need anyone to tell me which way the wind is blowing, and if the end has to come then I am determined it'll happen here, in my own home.

The priest who calls out of some duty on a weekly basis sits and drinks the cup of tea that Gina gives him, or the drop of something stronger if it's late enough, and he talks about heaven and what it's like there with a certainty he can't have possibly earned, answering all kinds of questions I haven't asked, going on as if death should be seen as a gift instead of something to be resisted for as long as possible. He's Father Crowley, a blow-in, ten years in Douglas but hailing originally from Clare, in a hamlet named Moyasta: a place so small, at least when he was young, that it took barely the length of a sneeze to pass through. I've never been a one for men of the cloth, and have always viewed them with suspicion, but I'll admit that I find Father Crowley a decent enough type. He has an easy-going way about him, middle-aged and I suppose at this point gone to seed – which is no harm at all in a priest, if it gets ungodly thoughts out of their heads. Gone to seed and, judging by how comfortable he seems around a glass of whiskey, I suspect going fast to pot. He's been peddling his heaven line for so long now that he has no choice but to keep it going, and to commit to it, but for me it's become background noise. Crickets. Not wanting to be rude, I let him finish his drink before closing my eyes, but I've already made up my mind that even if he's wrong and death proves nothing more than a perfect stillness, it won't matter. Whatever there is will be enough, because I've stopped thinking of death as an end. I sit with Bill, telling him about my growing up, about my father in the wars, or ghosts and fairies and the Banshee and the time of the Black and Tans, and seeing myself as he sees me I'm stunned to find this impossibly old woman, little more than sticks and rags of flesh, skin cracked and cobwebbed, and only barely recognisable. His eyes, if the light hits them just right, are the precise and very particular shade of my father's, a blue that is almost grey and at the same time almost green; and some of the mannerisms he has, the way he can't wear a shirt without roughly rolling the sleeves up past his elbows or how he pinches his lips when listening or lifts his chin before saying something he's been thinking about, combine to put Dinsy sitting all of a sudden before me again.

The tablets must have worked because I've slept deeply for the first time in days. I don't immediately open my eyes because I can't seem to, but I sense that I am not alone in the room and I know by the weight of the still-ness that my companion is May. I am breathing very slowly, and feel far away from myself. But May notices some stirring in me and asks in a small, careful voice, if I'm all right, if there's anything I need. For a moment I try not to move, because the pain has returned, worse than it's been for quite some time. The air feels ashy on my lips and tongue and leaves me in a shudder, and I finally look up to find the daylight almost gone and the room mired in dusk.

May gets up to help me into an armchair by the fire. She doesn't need strength to deal with me; I am feathers in her arms. The movement hurts in a new way, and when she raises me to my feet and leads me to the chair, holding me as if we were dancing, my eyes blur and I feel the cool spill of tears on my cheeks. She is not at all rough with me as she props me up with cushions and pulls the blanket around my shoulders, but when she looks at me, searching for new signs of deterioration, I tell her, with weariness rather than annoyance, to stop fussing. And once she is sure I'm all right, she returns to her own chair, beside me and barely an arm's reach away.

I've learned that it helps to keep still. After a few minutes the pain eases, though it leaves a cramp in the lower part of my stomach, and my breath finds as much ease as it ever does nowadays, so that I can finally talk in something like my usual voice.

'How late is it?' I ask, glancing at the window, the sky moiling behind the rain-beaded glass and fast running out of light.

'After five,' May says. 'You slept. I'm here an hour, and was just starting to wonder if you'd wake at all, if you might be down for the night. But you needed the rest. And you'll be in the better of it.'

The fire, the only semblance of proper brightness, keeps drawing my gaze, the red and orange glow of the cinders putting me in mind of what I used to glimpse when peering from across the road into the blackness of the old forge.

'Is Liam up?' I say, trying to remember if he has a shift tonight. My mind can't seem to decide, and I am anxious. Something has changed between this morning and now.

'Long 'go,' May says. 'They've all gone down to Quinnsworth for a few messages. Just to get out of the house, I think. The rain had Bill climbing the walls. And Gina wanted you to sleep.'

I nod, but don't respond. Quinnsworth is a super-market within a shopping centre that has done a lot to modernise Douglas, and I suppose to ease people's hard-ship. It has stood now for a decade or so, but my mind still sees it as the hay field it had forever been. When I did shop there, while I was still able, I thought about the long hot autumn days when all of Douglas would gather for the threshing, and the men would pass around bottles of cold milky tea whenever they paused for breath while the children played at climbing the haystacks or paddled in the river, clutching empty jam jars that they'd sneaked from their mothers' pantries and trying to catch thorneens and sprats. Those days are gone, but not for me.

Again, I have this sensation of floating in mist. I try to believe that it's the twilight, weakening now by the heartbeat towards full night, that has me feeling this way. But it's not.

'Nellie, are you all right? Is there anything you need – a cup of tea, a drop of something?'

'No,' I say, and I want to close my eyes and be once more where I was, in reassuring sleep, but I resist that pull, afraid that I might not so easily come back from there again. 'No, girl, I don't. Not a while. But I had a fierce mind for laughing earlier on, you know. Our poor father was over there by the door, sitting on a low stool and complaining about his feet, and when Annie put out a dish of water for him he was nearly scalded. His soldier's feet, he used to say. Remember? All the marching and the wading around in trenches, up to his shins in water half the time. Up to his oxters, he used to tell us.'

I drag my gaze from the light of the fire to look at May, and see that she is sitting forwards a little in her chair, watching me. I attempt a smile, for her benefit, and feel it ridiculous on my mouth, as if to say I recognise the nonsense I am spilling. Only, it's not nonsense at all. With the sight of them still fresh in my mind, I feel afraid, and saddened.

'That's just ghosts,' she says, from out of the silence. 'You know I see them myself, all the time. It's the mind playing tricks. At our age, we do nothing but remember.' But sensing, maybe, that I need more reassurance, she reaches out for my hand. Her skin is like paper, cool and smooth and very dry, and her fingers are as crooked as my own. 'Anyway,' she adds, 'isn't it a comfort to know they're never far from us?'

I smile again, still without meaning it, but by now the dusk has so thickened that the gesture goes unseen. I have more to say, more I want to talk about, such as how Annie had come right to my bedside and kissed my cheek, the whole moment so vivid that I could feel the mattress shifting when she pressed down on it with both hands, and how my father had remained in the doorway, tall and straight as he'd been in the best days I'd known him, decked out in his braces with the top two buttons of his collarless shirt undone, watching me without wavering while Annie promised they'd see me again soon, that it wouldn't be long now. And I want to tell May that though it was just my father and Annie who came to me, I was sure that I could hear our grandmother, Nancy, out in the hallway, singing something soft and very old and full of love, and I was given plenty of sense, without it needing to be said or shown, that the others were there too, and waiting. But I don't speak of these things, because such talk will only frighten her.

That's the second time in recent days that I've seen my dead, and the other had felt like more of a dream, because the encounter took place outside, in the long grass of the Hall Field behind our old backyard, with Annie, as she'd been when a girl of mid-teens, trying to teach me the steps to some dance that she herself was trying to perfect. My father, leaning with one hip against the wall that separated our yard from the field, and so that we had something to move to, singing 'The Black Velvet Band' as best he could, his baritone barely holding the melody, with my mother and an also young Mata alongside him clapping along in the rhythm of a quick waltz. The sun was shining and a light breeze was moving the grass around us, and there was a lot of good-natured laughter from Annie at my missteps, and it didn't seem at all strange to any of us that I was this crow of an old woman in my sister's arms instead of the young girl that I should by rights have been.

When I woke and Gina came to check on me, I told her in gasps that I hadn't wanted to come back from that dream, and she cried – for her a release long overdue. She's taken to drifting through days, keeping her hands busy with small chores but seeming otherwise out of tune with her surroundings. She needed to hear about the dream, and I needed to speak of it, though later on I tried to wave it away as nothing more than fantasy, wishful thinking, or some silliness brought on by the tablets and the whiskey. I know what I saw, I know where I was and who I was with, and the smallest details, down to the smell of the grass or the prickling of sweat on the backs of my bare legs, or the weighty hush of my father's breath through his singing or the sensation of the warm breeze pulling at Annie's long hair, these and dozens more that I could pluck from the moment, continue to feel entirely real. That I'd woken with the dancing still in mid-swing kept it all alive, and in my head Annie's voice has remained loud and laughing, assuring me that it would happen very easily and that they'd all be there, waiting.

I am used to sleeping in fits and starts, but these last few days I've been fighting to keep awake. And there's this thought rolling through my head, one I've heard priests recite many times: *no man knoweth the day or the hour*. I'm waiting, that's all, and time runs to its own pace. From my bed I hear my family's muted conversations, though not what's actually being said, and the hum of voices is enough, the different pitches as warming to me as the wash of the fire, these days and nights kept lit. The weather has turned bad, stormy, and the wind slams against the front of the house and sometimes calls out in the chimney, but feeling that the world has turned so ferocious somehow puts me at my ease, knowing how safe we all are inside. And when I do wake, whether for just a minute or for a little longer, the room around me is always the same. I've said my goodbyes, not in so many words but in ways that will make sense later on, when they each think back on these days. And there's not a lot more that needs saying.

Just now, somewhere above me, a toilet flushes, water runs, and then footsteps take the stairs, and everything feels slow and at a distance, lost in fog. When I lift myself back to consciousness I find yet another morning waiting, grained with the same storm that has been lashing us for days now without respite. And I see Liam, staring into space in the doorway, not looking at me until he notices me watching. It must be early because sleep is still on him, but he is dressed for the day to come in corduroy trousers and a tight-fitting V-necked jumper. Worry, and the trials of these past couple of years in particular, have put age into his expression. His black hair has grown longer than he likes and is starting to show a dusting of grey. Though this must be a rare day off, he's up early, I suppose unable to change the habits of a lifetime. He has a rolled cigarette between the tips of his thumb and finger, and when he notices me he seems somehow surprised to find me here and, after the slightest hesitation, nods a good morning. It's a small gesture, the barest tip of the head, but I am grateful enough for it, and I respond in kind.

'How are you feeling, Nellie?' he asks, and moves forward just a step so that he's clear of the hallway. Immediately, because of the space he's created, the bustle of the kitchen washes through, and to my surprise at this hour it is already full of people. Gina is asking about more tea, and my other children and their partners seem to have come to visit, and May, too, their voices easily identifiable even within the small racket of the breakfast conversation. But for just these few seconds, until we're noticed by the others, we can ignore their intrusion. 'Did you get any bit of sleep at all?'

With effort, I sit up. He starts towards me but I am still feeling the effects of my last injection, and I can manage.

'I did,' I tell him. 'But I'm not the one in need of it. I'll be asleep long enough.'

There's more I want to say, and that we might want to say to one another, but before we can, Bill comes charging through into the room, acting as the leading runner in an Olympic sprint. He is nimble as a fly, slipping between his father and the armchair, and turning without slowing he squeals with laughter and throws up his arms in victory, before vanishing again through the doorway, out into the hall and up the stairs.

After this the others, realising I am awake, drift through from the kitchen, carrying mugs of tea. Gina is last into the room, with Martin in her arms; Liam has moved, ahead of the new arrivals, to take up a position at the side of the fire, and his and my daughter's eyes briefly meet across the small huddle of bodies that keeps them apart, but the smile she tries for falls away all too quickly. She has washed her face and the fringe of her hair is still damp and clinging to her forehead, but she seems dazed, as if having just woken. She eases her way past the others and, though there is no need yet, drops to one knee in front of the fire and adds a brick of turf and a few lumps of coal to all that is already burning. Then she comes and sits beside me on the bed, and takes my hand, playing the cool dry skin of her fingers against my palm.

At ease again, I settle back down on my pillow and, smiling at her, close my eyes.

Acknowledgements

This book owes its existence to a number of people:

My editors Robin Robertson and Daisy Watt deserve my deepest thanks, for pushing me in such relentless fashion to get it into decent fighting shape. Any lingering errors are due to stubbornness on my part. Daisy encouraged me to try for better, and then better again, even when I probably thought I'd done enough; and it's because of Robin, and the opportunities he's given me, that I am no longer toiling in such obscurity.

Special thanks are due also to everyone at Jonathan Cape and Vintage, from those involved with the design all the way through to the rights and sales staff. Their efforts give a story like *Life Sentences* a chance in the world, a place on the shelves of bookshops and hopefully a place in the hands of readers.

One intense and critical round of redrafting was undertaken during a month-long stay as writer-in-residence at KU Leuven's Irish College, at the invitation of Hedwig

Schwall, director of the Leuven Centre for Irish Studies. Hedwig and her husband Mel ensured I saw all the wonders that Belgium had to offer, everything from Waterloo to the Flanders fields, and along with their housemate Rob kept me (and fellow scribe and pub companion, Rosemary Jenkinson, who was also at the time in residence) wonderfully fed, wined and regaled.

The support of my family was critical. My parents Liam and Gina have always been open books for me, and right from the beginning constant as the stars in their support of my writing. For that, I will always be grateful. I am thankful, also, to my brother Martin, his wife Kate, the wild ones, Liam and Ellen, and the wildest one of all, Jazz.

What's here in *Life Sentences* is a skin of fiction laid over a considerable amount of fact and truth drawn from things I'd been told over the years. For a lot of the rest, I relied on the able (and sometimes jawdropping) research carried out by Yann and my sister Irene. I'm not sure they anticipated that I'd put their trawling to quite this use, but they'll know better next time.